# D. B. COOPER
## -aftermath-

A Novel by

## GENE ELMORE

iUniverse, Inc.
New York   Bloomington

Copyright © 2010 by Gene Elmore

All rights reserved. No part of this book may be used or reproduced by any means, graphic, electronic, or mechanical, including photocopying, recording, taping or by any information storage retrieval system without the written permission of the publisher except in the case of brief quotations embodied in critical articles and reviews.

This novel is a work of fiction interwoven with the facts and people present when a man identifying himself as Dan Cooper jumped from an airliner in 1971. Except for all of the characters in the opening chapter and four characters in later chapters, Anna Song, Dona Elliott, her son Jack and Brian Ingran, any resemblance to actual persons is coincidental.

iUniverse books may be ordered through booksellers or by contacting:

iUniverse
1663 Liberty Drive
Bloomington, IN 47403
www.iuniverse.com
1-800-Authors (1-800-288-4677)

Because of the dynamic nature of the Internet, any Web addresses or links contained in this book may have changed since publication and may no longer be valid. The views expressed in this work are solely those of the author and do not necessarily reflect the views of the publisher, and the publisher hereby disclaims any responsibility for them.

ISBN: 978-1-4502-1545-9 (sc)
ISBN: 978-1-4502-1546-6 (ebook)

Printed in the United States of America

iUniverse rev. date: 04/26/2010

This novel is a work of fiction interwoven with the facts and people present when a man identifying himself as Dan Cooper jumped from an airliner in 1971. Except for all of the characters in the opening chapter and four characters in later chapters, *Anna Song, Dona Elliott, her son Jack and Brian Ingran,* any resemblance to actual persons is coincidental.

Also by Gene Elmore

## THE TURNAROUND

Based on fact, and his travels to the Middle East while flying for the Navy. THE TURNAROUND spans several decades to tell the story about an Iranian terrorist. Mike Tolson, the Managing Editor of a national news network has an unshakable faith that always held steady except for one mistake for which his wife faces the retaliation. The plot twists and turns with increasing intensity to a startling conclusion offering an inspiring message.

One Review: I have never read an international thriller, novel that ends on such an upbeat note. I particularly enjoyed your obvious extensive knowledge of international relations and of Iran, particularly.

Paul B. Dean, M. D.

# ABOUT THE AUTHOR

As a Naval Aviator, an Engineer and business owner, Gene Elmore traveled the world and saw first hand much that is described in his writing. He seeks to provide a spiritual dynamic experience that enlightens and entertains.

# ACKOWLEDGMENTS

To my wife, Wanda, the first to read the manuscript, for her encouragement in all the things I do —a delightful person with values we should all emulate.

To a special friend, Steve Greene, a published author who rode a tricycle pulling a trailer from Oregon to the heart of Death Valley. He designed and produced the art work for the cover and assisted me in so many ways to publish D. B. Cooper –aftermath–.

To my friend, Terry Shanklin, who said to me, "You know, Gene, you should write a book about the return of D. B. Cooper." That's how it all started. The ideas began to flow. After three trips to Oregon and Washington and attending three of the annual celebrations in Ariel, Washington, the book is complete.

To my son, James who suggested that Ted Bolan could be a retired CIA agent.

# The Beginning

At 4:45 p.m. on the night before Thanksgiving in 1971 Northwest Orient's Flight 305, a Boeing 727, the only airliner with a rear stairwell to enter the cabin lifted from a wet runway and nosed up into a low dense overcast. Breaking out above the clouds, long streaks of light in the west were about to create a memorable sunset. With only thirty-six passengers and no food service on this short flight from Portland to Seattle, the two flight attendants had time to mingle with the passengers.

Florence Schaffner had already noticed the quiet man in a business suit and tinted glasses in 15D, an aisle seat near the rear of the aircraft. When he handed her a folded piece of paper, she slipped it into her pocket without reading it thinking he was attempting to make time with her. She was quite nice—shapely—and used to men, away from their wives for a night, making passes at her.

Moments later, as she passed in the aisle, she heard him say, "Read it." At the rear of the plane, standing next to her colleague, she opened the note. "My God, Tina, look at this."

Tina Mucklow read the note. "Oh boy."

The note was printed in ink. The exact wording will never be known since the man later insisted that it be returned. It said that he had a bomb in the case beside him. He wanted $200,000 in twenty dollar bills and four parachutes to be delivered to him when the plane landed in Seattle.

Florence Schaffner went forward with the note in hand.
"It has to be a hoax," Captain William W. Scott said.
"I don't think so," she said.

Scott left first officer, Bill Rataczak, at the controls. The man had moved to 15F, a window seat. The briefcase laid on his lap. Scott sat down next to him. In a low voice, he asked, "What's this about a bomb?"

The man opened the case and then closed it. Scott had seen two red cylinders and a mass of wires. "I'm perfectly serious, Captain."

"He had piercing black eyes behind tinted glasses," Captain Scott said later. "He instructed me to remain in the air over Seattle until arrangements to comply with his requests had been completed. Most passengers didn't even know about a hijacking—just the inconvenience of a routine delay before landing."

Northwest's terminal manager in Portland, Frank Faist, called the airline's headquarters. It was close to seven o'clock in Minneapolis when he reached Northwest's President, Donald W. Nyrop at home. Some hard decisions had to be made fast. After a few quick phone calls, he issued the order. "Do whatever the man demands."

With a lot of scurrying around the FBI prepared the ten thousand twenty dollar bills. Time did not permit putting together a package of bills bearing consecutive serial numbers. However, several steps were taken to make identification of the money as easy as possible. All 10,000 twenties had serial numbers beginning with *L*, a code letter indicating that they had been issued at San Francisco. Most were *Series 1969-C*, another recognizable tag. All of the bills were run through a high speed Recordak machine to photograph and place every bill on microfilm. Sometime later the images would be sorted into serial number order and distributed to banks coast to coast.

From the Recordak machine, the bills were stacked in decks of 100, paper taped and packed in a canvas moneybag. The bundle was the size and weight of two large phone books. A Seattle police car took the money and raced over wet streets to the airport, siren howling.

Another patrol car sped through the streets transporting four parachutes provided by the Issaquah Skydiving School.

The tower advised Captain Scott, "We are ready down here."

Flight 305 landed. The hijacker's instructions, delivered verbally by Tina Mucklow to Captain Scott, were explicit: "Taxi to an empty well-lighted area of the airport. The planes interior lights are to be kept low. All who approach the plane must do so on foot one at a time."

Captain Scott obediently taxied to a bright floodlighted area not far from the administration building. He sent Tina into the cabin with some questions.

She sat down next to the lone bandit. "The Captain wants to know about the passengers. Can they go?"

"Yes, get them off the plane," he said. "Use the aft stairs."

"And the crew?"

"No, I want them to stay on board."

"All of us?"

"The two pilots and you. We have some flying to do."

"Me?"

A rapport had developed between these two. Tina Mucklow would have been uneasy if, looking into his eyes, she saw signs of agitation or hostility. She saw none of this. By her very nature she always tried to be a young lady of quality and dignity. She was twenty-two, tall and attractive.

"He wasn't nervous," Tina told questioners later. "He seemed rather nice and never cruel or nasty—a man in his forties with a Bing Crosby look—thoughtful and calm."

When the passengers were gone, Tina came back through the empty cabin with another message. "The four parachutes are here. They are in a Northwest courier cart. How close will you let it come?"

The man reminded Tina that only one man at a time could walk to the plane. She was to station herself at the foot of the aft stairs and take the parachutes.

She watched as he examined the chutes. "Are you going to make somebody else jump?" With only one, it would have been easy to supply a faulty chute.

"Maybe," he replied.

The same courier cart returned with the canvas bag containing the L bills.

Captain William W. Scott, a twenty-year veteran with Northwest Orient Airlines, was instructed to fly south, stay below 170 knots (196 miles per hour) at ten thousand feet with the landing gear down and no pressurization. With no pressurization the pressure inside and outside the aircraft is the same and, at ten thousand feet, people can breathe normally. Also, there is no problem opening doors. "Tell the Captain I am wearing a skydiver's altimeter on my wrist," the skyjacker told Tina.

Because of mountains, only one route existed between Seattle and Reno where an airplane could fly safely at that altitude. The lone hijacker had designated that route. The rear stairwell exit below the tail must remain unlocked.

After takeoff, Tina Mucklow was instructed to go forward to the flight deck, close the door and not return until after landing in Reno. A light on the engineer's panel indicated when the stairwell opened.

Captain Scott called on the intercom loudspeaker. "Is there anything we can do for you?"

Then the single word response, "no." That was the last word ever heard from the man called D. B. Cooper. Just seconds later the airplane performed a slight curtsy that Captain Scott had never experienced before.

*D.B. Cooper -aftermath-*

The FBI later reported that the man exited the rear stairs with two chutes: a backpack and a chest pack. The chest pack had been a dummy that the Issaquah Skydiving School used for instructional purposes in the classroom. In the haste of the moment it had been inadvertently taken from the shelf. The backpack was a good, professionally packed chute.

Earl Cossey, the master rigger from the Issaquah Skydiving School that supplied the parachutes, stated that this jump was not a foolhardy stunt. An experienced jumper could do it with a reasonable assurance of success. He volunteered to re-enact the jump but liability problems with the airline's insurance would not allow this.

There were doubts as to whether a man could even walk down the open stairwell. The slipstream of the aircraft in flight only permitted the stairs to drop a foot or so below the closed position. A young FBI agent, wearing two chutes for safety, duplicated the same conditions. He walked to the bottom step. His weight caused the stairs to drop to the open position. "Though extremely windy it was not difficult at all," he reported.

A two hundred pound sled, with a rope attached, was allowed to slide down the stairs. The stairs opened when the sled neared the bottom, just as it had before with the young FBI agent. When the sled dropped, the stairs returned to a near closed position and the same curtsy that Captain Scott had reported—the same momentary dip of the aircraft's nose that had been recorded on the plane's flight recorder—had been reproduced. This is how investigators determined the spot where he jumped.

Today, in Ariel, Washington the name, D. B. Cooper, is emblazoned in large red, white and blue letters above the entrance of the only store in town. The storeowner displays memorabilia throughout the year and has a special celebration on the Saturday following Thanksgiving commemorating his crime. People and reporters come from miles around to commemorate the incident. Some of the local people say they know who he is but none really do.

A man the press identified as D. B. Cooper became the first successful hijacker of an airliner. Only the Captain and the two Flight Attendants ever spoke to the man. He bailed out over Ariel, Washington, thirty-five miles north of Portland. Even though the authorities determined the exact spot where he jumped, they never found a trace of him. Ten years later a small boy found $5,880 of old decayed money with the serial numbers Cooper stole on that dark night.

Throughout the United States people smile when they hear his name. Many view the crime as a feat, both cunning and daring. Now, almost thirty years later, a new story is about to begin.

# THE IDEA EMERGES

Ted Bolan berated himself on losing his house slippers. The old polished wood floor felt cold to his bare feet as he made his way through the kitchen to the wooden country-style table and chairs. Now 78, he liked the warmth of the old dinette set. The house was a hundred years old. He and Molly had remodeled it with early 20th century decor and many antiques. He glanced through the huge bay window overlooking the lush Tacoma valley and waters of Puget Sound two hundred feet below.

His home computer, the homepage set to CNN.com, was always on and ready to go with access, not only to CNN but also to any newspaper in the world, free of charge—no furniture ads. But Ted liked the feel of the morning paper almost as much as he craved his morning cup of dark roast coffee. The automatic timer had already started the brewing and the smell of fresh perking java restored his amiable mood. He leisurely scanned headlines and turned pages. A news item on page six caught his attention.

**Senator Jay Donovan to be Honored**

The senior Senator from Oregon, Jay Donovan, 56, will be honored at a celebration at the Windoff Country Club in Portland on October 18th for his 25th year in the Senate. Marilyn

Donovan, 31, his wife of three years, will accompany him.

Being an ex-CIA field operative, long since retired, Ted knew about discretion, political correctness, political fallout and media leaks which were more often intentional than accidental. The Senator was a first class con man. In addition to being an alcoholic, most of the time functional, Jay Donovan had once been formally accused of murdering his first wife and then a doctor mysteriously changed her testimony and the charges were dropped. The Senator had a way of fixing things. Two days after the inquest, the doctor, her car and some of her belongings disappeared never to be heard from again. She had just packed up and left.

How the Senator was able to afford his lavish lifestyle was an even bigger mystery and many people believed rival press leaks that implied Donovan was involved in illegal drug trafficking. Why do the voters keep electing him? Ted wondered, squirming in his chair.

There was more that Ted Bolan remembered. Senator Jay Donovan, on more than one occasion had been directly responsible for consorting with terrorists and thereby compromising Ted and his team of intelligence agents, placing them in mortal danger after they had already crossed into unfriendly territory. Even after Ted retired from the CIA, he was convinced that there were times when the FBI should have stepped in with a firm hand but they didn't. He suspected the Senator had close ties with Steve Bowers, the current FBI Director.

Footsteps creaked through the old hardwood as Molly came down the stairs and then came the familiar shuffle of soft leather house slippers as she ambled into the kitchen to the breakfast nook. She kissed her husband's thinning hairline before getting coffee. Even though she was past seventy, her youthful figure still excited him.

"I think I'll just have fruit this morning," she said. "Can I get you anything?"

"I was going to make us a couple of omelets."

"Why don't you fix one for yourself? I'm just not that hungry."

Ted knew that Molly had always been as envious of his good physical condition as he was of her ability to always know where to find her house slippers. She reached over to the kitchen counter and flipped the small TV on before slipping into the breakfast nook with two cups of coffee. NEWDAY, CBS's morning show hosted by Karen Dyer, would be starting. She was a favorite, a beauty that Ted liked. He and Molly watched, at first confused and then shocked.

"My God, Ted, that's the World Trade Center."

"It sure is." He grabbed the remote to turn the volume up.

Smoke billowed on all sides completely obliterating the top twenty floors of the tall structure that Ted had frequented so many times in years past, one of a pair of skyscrapers towering above all other buildings. Ted and Molly stared, not believing, when they saw the airliner approaching fast—slamming into the second tall structure. The building didn't move—not a quiver—smoke and fire flared in a series of explosions half way down. They moved into the family room to the larger TV and did not budge for the next three hours watching one commentator after the next offer analysis of the tragedy. Then, Senator Jay Donovan came on.

Watching the Senator, having just read about the celebration of his twenty-fifth year in the Senate, Ted began to evolve a plan to put the Senator in a position of extortion. Ted was forever coming up with plausible schemes, which were in fact, part of his former job in the CIA—creating scenarios, acting them out, discovering weaknesses and coming up with stronger defenses. And the sweetest revenge would place millions of the Senator's blood money directly into the Ted Bolan Foundation. No one would never suspect him. He'd do it alone. His years of experience had taught him that perfect crimes should always be the act of one person. *No leaks that way.*

Now, after the World Trade Center disaster, he could direct the funds toward relief efforts for the victims. *Fifty thousand people are in those two towers.* The Senator and all his attorneys couldn't stop it. The irony of such a plan hit him. In a sense, he would be setting things right by using the Senator as a pawn to aid victims of a catastrophe not of their making.

*I'll go to Ariel Washington and then Portland, Oregon. After that I'll go to New York to solicit Karen Dyer's help.* Her journalistic prowess would be essential to carry out his plan. He'd need a ploy to get through to her. *The hijacking in 1971—she grew up in Seattle and she'd know about D. B. Cooper—that would do it.* He also needed four cell phones. He'd buy those in New York as far away from Washington and Oregon as he could get. *I'll take Molly with me.* There were some things to do before New York.

Ted's workshop was above the garage. Here, he created the tools of his hobby, ventriloquism, a collection of dummies. For Ted, they were anything but dumb. Elsie and Max were his favorites. He'd use those two at the officer installation party of the local VFW chapter this coming Saturday night. He had been the master of ceremonies at the annual event for years—ever since his retirement from the CIA fifteen years ago.

# The Party

Three hundred members and guests milled about at the VFW installation party, talking, standing, sitting, eating, drinking and having a good time. The affair was not a formal dinner but an extended cocktail party with hearty hors d'oeuvres of broccoli with a cream cheese/dill dip and baby shrimp with spicy cocktail sauce. Red, white and blue streamers were draped across the ceiling. Brightly decorated centerpieces adorned every table.

Barely a hundred hours had passed since the World Trade Center tragedy and the rhetoric ran hot and heavy. Veterans and friends, caught up in the festivities, took turns at the microphone telling stories, expressing patriotic feelings, or offering simple prayers for the country in a time of great despair.

Ted kept the party on schedule by injecting his own blend of timely humor and sympathy with Elsie on one knee and Max on the other. Then, casting Elsie and Max aside, he began impersonating famous personalities. The crowd responded with hearty laughter and applause as he changed from one character to the next—a welcome release after the World Trade Center catastrophe. With his body language and voice, the audience envisioned Jack Benny, Bob Hope and Jimmy Durante.

The bartender prepared fresh drinks for two VFW members chuckling as they watched Ted on stage at the far side of the large room. "With that artificial nose, he looks like Jimmy

Durante," the younger member said. "How many characters can he do?"

"He never runs out of material," the older member said without taking his eyes off the stage where Ted was performing. "He has a collection of noses and face masks—makes all of his own stuff. You should hear him do Ronald Reagan. That's his best."

The bartender finished mixing their drinks. The old-timer wrapped a cocktail napkin around his gin and tonic and raised it to take a sip.

"It's hard to believe he's past seventy," the younger member said reaching for his drink.

"He's pushing 80. He was a Navy pilot flying B24 Liberators in WWII when he and I joined this post in 1946. Never saw much of him after that until he returned to Tacoma following his retirement from the CIA. He still has an airplane."

"Sounds like he had an interesting career."

"Yeah, he really did. He was on the Tacoma City Council for eight years after his return. He spearheaded the forming of our VFW Foundation to build the first Homeless Refuge for Kids. It's named *The Ted Bolan Foundation* in his honor. There, listen, he's doing Ronald Reagan."

"My God, sounds just like him—even looks like him, with that sloppy hat," the younger member said reaching for another napkin to put around his cold glass.

"Ted needs to be a couple inches taller. Reagan's over six foot."

~~~~~

"You were good tonight," Molly said as they drove home from the party.

The top was down and the chilly September air whipped over the windshield of the small MG sports car. Ted had restored it and he liked to drive it when by himself or just the two of them. He wasn't driving fast. The air rippled through Molly's shoulder length blond hair like a whipping flag.

"Yeah, it was fun. Always is." His hand nestled in her hand.

"You know what makes the VFW Post so great, honey? You guys all like each other and you have integrity."

He smiled. *Integrity* and *me planning a crime.* "Did you read the paper this morning, that short blurb about Jay Donovan?"

"The celebration of his twenty-fifth year in the Senate—isn't that awful? The more he lies, the more people applaud him."

"He has a lot of underworld connections and he corrupts a lot of people. He's good at what he does."

"I still think he killed his first wife and he has so much money."

Ted turned into their driveway and punched the garage door button. "Yeah, he sure does."

# The Preparation

Eight days after the VFW Installation party and just under four weeks before the Senator's anniversary celebration, Ted Bolan drove to Ariel, Washington north of Portland located on a tributary feeding into the Columbia River. Ariel was just a spot on the map—290 people and one store with a tin roof. Dona Elliott and her son, Jack owned it. Ted dropped in to say hello—he had not seen them since the last annual D. B. cooper celebration in November 2000.

He continued east another five miles before stopping to start his search at a place where a gravel drive should be. Large pines, firs, hemlocks and cedars towered against the sky. The ground was immersed in dark green shadows with a mass of weeds three feet high. He remembered a derelict cabin back off the road. He knew it was there but where? It had been years since he last saw it. Even then, it had been abandoned for a long time. An old gravel driveway grown over with weeds had dead-ended at the door. He searched. The minutes passed. Then he saw the small concrete stoop buried in undisturbed heavy growth. The door stood ajar—cobwebs, spiders and dust everywhere. The old cabin had a single room with a sink at one end, a commode in one corner and no partitions or ceiling. Spanner logs every few feet tied the log roof rafters together.

A pungent smell made him sneeze as he swept the spider webs aside. He wouldn't repair the sink or commode. The gravel drive with its overgrown weeds was hardly passable but his truck would make it okay. He'd have to be careful not to make too many trips that would create signs of use.

He returned to his pickup truck and made some notes. The plywood he required would have to be light enough that he could handle the panels. Half-inch would do it. He'd cut every piece to size so that no additional sawing would be necessary. The concrete floor in the old cabin was old and cracked but adequate—nothing necessary for that.

The only power requirements would be a single low wattage light bulb and keeping two cell phones charged. Two deep cycle batteries, the kind they use in motor homes, boats and golf carts would do the job.

≈≈≈≈

The next day in Portland he scouted out some used-car lots featuring older cars. He didn't go in—he just wanted to know where they were. A salvage yard, on the north side of Portland, was listed. He called the number. "I'm looking for an old clunker that still runs good," he told the man.

"Most of the stuff we get is towed in. We get one once in a while that still runs," the man said.

"Fine, I'll check with you later."

That afternoon, a Thursday, he followed an armored truck and watched the men make their rounds. He had to know what kind of accounts the armored truck would pick up on the day following the Senator's party. Most of all, he needed to know the truck's final destination and the time it would arrive. He watched the door rise at the rear of the Federal Bank. The armored truck entered and the door closed. The bank fronted on a large parking lot shared by a Wal-Mart. A Chevron station and some other small businesses were across a street. The intersection of Dayton and Ratcliff Streets was two blocks away—*a good place for Karen Dyer and crew to stand by.* He found a motel nearby but did not go in.

Driving north on Interstate 5 he pulled off at the La Center exit, twenty-four miles north of Portland. La Center, Washington was two miles off the freeway. He knew the area. Molly had lived near Ariel, just ten miles away, when he met her. He parked and went into the only hardware store in town. He needed to know if Rufus was still around.

Manikins were sitting here and there, not for sale, just décor, some standing, others sitting, all life sized. The store was famous for them—had been for fifty years. Two youngsters, a boy and a girl sitting on a park bench, a take-off of a Norman Rockwell painting, stood in one corner where it had been as long as Ted could remember. Another Rockwell—the little girl and the doctor taking the doll's temperature was on the other side of the old store. Like everything else in the old store, the manikins needed to be dusted.

Dewey, the proprietor sat behind the counter dozing in an old overstuffed armchair. It, too, had been there as long as Ted could remember. Waiting at the counter for the old man to wake up, Ted finally rang the bell next to the cash register.

The old man awoke with a start and slowly rose to his feet before ambling to the counter. Not yet making eye contact, he said, "Good morning. What can I do for you?"

Dewey had aged so much in the five years since Ted saw him last. "Do you remember me?" Ted said.

Slowly, slipping his wire-framed glasses down from his forehead with shaking hands, Dewey looked at Ted's face and said, "Yeah, I remember you. You're Ted Bolan."

"It's been a long time, five or six years maybe."

"Seems like yesterday. Are you still on the City Council in Tacoma?"

Nothing wrong with the old man's mind, Ted thought. "No, I gave that up five years ago. Rufus still making manikins for you?"

"He brings a new one in every year or so. I think I'm the only one he makes them for now. He can't work like he use to."

Rufus, a Hispanic man, started making custom lifelike manikins in his garage as a young man. Stores throughout Oregon and Washington commissioned him. Dewey used them to create an atmosphere—a special décor to attract customers.

He offered Ted a beer. The two of them reminisced about days long gone. Nothing much had changed, just the two of them becoming older.

After leaving the hardware store, Ted checked the casino parking lot across the street—*a good place to park my van on the day after the Senator's party.*

Going north another half-mile, Ted turned right onto a two-lane county road. He checked his odometer. At one mile the county road curved left into an area of tall trees and uncut foliage. Past the curve he found the turnoff veering to the left, overgrown with underbrush just as he remembered it—a good place to hide a car with enough space to park a second car. He'd need a life-sized dummy of an old woman sitting in the front seat, a change of clothes, bib overalls, a shirt, old shoes, a straw hat and a Rufus ID for that car.

≈≈≈≈≈

The western sky glowed with a brilliant orange over a setting sun when Ted arrived home in Tacoma. The van was gone. Molly was probably out shopping. He entered the garage and climbed the stairs to his shop to make sketches and list the required materials. In addition to his dark clothes, he'd need three black felt hoods. One of them would have eyeholes and be contoured to fit over his glasses for comfort and good vision. He'd be wearing that one for several hours.

In two weeks he'd go to New York. He'd need identification, a New York driver's license with a picture. He opened a file drawer and retrieved a folder with Id's he had used in years past before retiring from the CIA. He had almost thrown it out a time or two but it didn't take up much space. Thumbing through the file, he found the one he was looking for, a license made out to a Norman Gilman with a New York address with Ted's picture. It had long since expired but that would be easy to fix. The picture was twenty years old but not that good and he hadn't changed that much.

He also needed an ID for Old Rufus. A well-worn Washington driver's license with a picture of himself, made up as a Hispanic, would do it. *That will be easy to do.* Two days before the Senator's party, he'd return to Portland and Ariel to complete the preparations.

He heard Molly pull into the driveway. Ted came down the stairs and walked toward the van as she eased to a stop.

"How'd it go in Portland?" she said, stepping out and opening the rear door.

"Fine." He reached into the van to get some of her purchases. "Dewey still has the hardware store. He asked about you and wished you well."

"Dona still running the store?"

"Yeah, she and her son Jack."

"Still lots of D. B. Cooper memorabilia?"

He smiled. "She's added to it. It's more cluttered than ever."

Molly grabbed a sack and started toward the house—Ted followed. They placed the bags on the kitchen counter.

"Why don't we plan a trip to New York to visit Tom and Mary, before the holidays?" He saw her smile. She and Mary had been close. Ted and Tom had been in the CIA together for thirty years.

"It would be fun to see Tom and Mary again. They'll want us to stay with them. Are we going to take the Bonanza?"

"No . . . it's too slow. Let's use the airline."

"Do you think they're safe?"

"With all the beefed up security, they're safer now than before and private flying is virtually shut down."

# GETTING READY

Molly enjoyed the comfort of the first-class seating. She closed her magazine and glanced at her watch. They would land in New York City within the next few minutes. The pressure had built up in her ears. Holding her nose with her mouth closed she blew the way Ted had taught her to do it. Her ears popped and the rumble of the engines became louder.

Ted closed his book and looked out the window. "It'll be good to see Tom and Mary again."

While still looking at Ted, she smiled and remembered. Tom had retired from the CIA two years after she and Ted returned to Tacoma. She looked forward to spending a few days with Mary in their home in the suburbs of New York City. They were waiting at the baggage claim area.

≈≈≈≈

The following day, at Tom and Mary's home, Karen Dyer's morning show, NEWDAY, had just ended. Today would be a good time to find out how much trouble he'd have reaching her, Ted thought. He had already looked up CBS's phone number and he needed to test it—make sure it was correct and find the best way to reach her. Most of all, he had to make the initial contact with her. He'd have to do it on a public phone.

"I have some shopping to do," Mary said to Molly. "Wanna go with me?"

"Sounds good to me," Molly said. "You guys want to come along?"

"Let's go with them, Tom."

Upon arriving at the mall, the women became engrossed in the shopping. Ted and Tom were browsing when Ted saw a bank of phone booths across the mall. "Tom, I need to make a phone call, I won't be long."

"I'll be right here."

Ted strolled across the mall and entered a phone booth. Nobody was around so he didn't bother closing the door. He entered CBS's phone number. The phone rang twice.

"This is CBS."

Ted smiled. *How nice to get a live operator.* "May I speak to Karen Dyer?" he said, using a raspy voice—the one he had chosen for this call.

"I'll ring her office."

He waited and closed the phone booth door as a stranger stepped into the adjoining booth.

"This is Karen Dyer's office."

"Tell her, this is D. B. Cooper."

"May I ask what this is regarding, Mr. Cooper?"

*The fame of D. B. Cooper had faded.* "Yes, just tell Miss Dyer that my name is D. B. Cooper and it's about a crime I will commit in a few weeks. It's a breaking story that she will be a part of."

"Ahh . . . just . . . just a moment."

He waited and remembered the time when he had met Karen Dyer some ten years ago. Like now, he and Molly were visiting New York. They attended Tom's Rotary Club meeting where Karen Dyer had been the speaker. She was twenty-five then.

At the Rotary meeting Karen Dyer had spoken about her ambition to become an overseas correspondent: "Women need to be able to take care of themselves if they want to be on a par with the men," she had said. She described her completion of a survival school, four weeks of intensive training where she had been the only woman. They had taught her about weapons, karate and how to endure interrogations in a harsh environment. "A graduation from hell," she had called it.

"Good morning, Mr. Cooper. This is Karen Dyer. How may I help you?"

"Miss Dyer, in a few weeks I am going to call you on this number and solicit your help to commit a crime."

"You're going to what?"

"I need your help to pull it off."

"What makes you think I'll do it?"

"You'll do it—you won't have a choice."

"Ha . . . I'll report this to authorities as soon as we hang up."

"That's exactly what I want you to do. I assume you're recording this call."

"I hit the record button as I answered. Are you the D. B. Cooper who jumped out of the airplane?"

*She does know about it.* "I remember when he did it."

"That was thirty years ago."

"The night before Thanksgiving in 1971. You would have been five at the time and you lived in Seattle." Ted saw Tom standing at the far side of the mall talking to someone. The man in the adjoining booth had the phone clamped against his ear peering through the glass. A man with two small children passed by.

"D. B. Cooper was reported to be in his forties," she said.

"That's right."

"Are you going to hijack another airliner?"

"I'll call you when I'm ready. I'm looking forward to meeting you again."

"We've met before?"

Tom was strolling toward the phone booths. "You were the speaker at a local Rotary club ten years ago. You described your graduation from hell."

"Survival school!"

"Yes. Good-bye, Miss Dyer."

After hanging up, Ted's thoughts continued to fill his mind. Karen Dyer had been a four-year employee with CBS, just 25 years old at the time of the Rotary meeting, a cub reporter endearing herself to her New York audience—*a slim voluptuous figure with penetrating brown eyes, a lovely face and curly auburn hair reaching her shoulders.*

She did become an overseas correspondent covering lively issues and frequently interviewing heads of state. After becoming Co-Host of CBS's NEWDAY show she continued to push timely events when she took on the drug dealers. She titled it, THE DRUG LORDS IN SOUTH AMERICA. The campaign lasted almost a year. She had managed to get an interview with the suspected kingpin—a man named Rostel Barstelli—a large man with a Clark Gable appearance. Some of her questions provided leads that led to arrests. Trials were pending. Barstelli fled to his villa somewhere in South America to avoid arrest.

*She is the perfect choice to provide the coverage I need to get Donovan's money.*

≈≈≈≈

As Karen Dyer hung up she looked at her pad where she had scribbled *D. B. Cooper—a crime in a few weeks—my support—you'll do it—exactly what I want.*

She knew about the annual celebration in Ariel, Washington every year on the Saturday following Thanksgiving. She had been raised in Seattle. *Is it really D. B. Cooper or some kind of a nut? He'd be past seventy. This has to be a hoax.* She pressed the intercom button. "Get Biff Roberts on the phone."

She had known Biff Roberts since her first days at CBS fresh out of San Diego State. He was the Assistant Director in Charge of the FBI New York Field Office responsible for conducting criminal and counterintelligence investigations within the five boroughs of New York City, a position he had held for ten years. Occasions arose when she had him on her show as a guest.

"Mr. Roberts is on the line," her secretary reported.

"Biff, I just received a call from a man who identified himself as D. B. Cooper. He said he's going to call me in a few weeks to solicit my help to commit a crime."

"The D. B. Cooper who jumped out of an airplane?"

"Who knows?"

"And he thinks you'll do it?"

"Biff, his exact words were, 'you'll do it—you won't have a choice.'"

"Do you think he's serious?"

"He sounded serious."

Ten minutes later Biff called back. "The call came from a public phone in the Landale shopping center. Be careful."

# THE CELL PHONES

Ted needed four cell phones. He had already perused the New York yellow pages and selected a company with a retail sales office in the Landale shopping center, the same center they were in a few hours ago. It was Friday. He and Molly would go home Tuesday. Tom and Mary were out on some personal business.

"Come on, Molly, I saw an ice-cream store this morning. I'll buy you a sundae and we can browse for a while." He knew she'd be easy to duck for an hour or so.

He wore an open collar and left his blazer in the car. He replaced his thin-rimmed aviation trifocals with heavy black-framed reading glasses that he had just purchased in a drug store. He had also purchased a New York Yankees baseball cap.

"May I help you?" the lady behind the sales counter asked when he entered the cell phone store.

With the same raspy voice he had used with Karen Dyer, he said, "I need four digital cellular phones that are programmable."

"We can program them while you wait. How much area do you want covered?"

"The United States."

"Alaska and Hawaii?"

"No, just the forty eight states. Program three of the four phones for incoming calls only—no outgoing calls."

"You can do that yourself by using your password."

"Why don't you do that for me?"

"I can do that."

"Your ad stated that your phones have a timer and that most all functions are programmable. I want to control the length of each call and the time before another call can be received on one of those phones."

The lady smiled. "You must have a teenager at home," and then added, "we can do that too. Calls will terminate after a set period of time."

"Program one phone to terminate all calls after sixty seconds and not receive another call for one hour."

She entered the information on an order form. "Charging cradles for your home or office are included. There is also a charging cable that can be plugged into the cigarette lighter in your car. If you sign up for service for one year, you'll receive a ten-percent discount. We do require a deposit."

"That's fine. I'll pay cash to cover the deposit and the first two months." He gave his name as Norman Gilman and presented the phony license he had placed in his wallet.

After returning to his car, Ted inspected the four cell phones to be sure their numbers were identified on each instrument. Then he labeled the only phone that could make outgoing calls #1. That one would be his phone.

The three phones, programmed for incoming calls only, were designated 2, 3 and 4. The one that terminated all calls after sixty seconds was number 2. He listed the four phone numbers on his appointment calendar and checked to be sure they rang properly and that he had not copied a wrong number. He programmed the numbers of phones #2, 3 and 4 into the automatic dial on phone #1, the one he would use. Then he walked across the parking lot to the bus station.

*D.B. Cooper -aftermath-*

He wiped phone #4 and placed it in public storage locker 102. He listed the locker and phone number on his appointment calendar.

He tossed the locker key in a trashcan and strolled out to meet Molly.

# The Time Had Come

The Senator's party would take place tomorrow. Since his retirement from the CIA Molly had become accustomed to knowing just about everything Ted did from one day to the next.

"I wish you'd tell me what you're doing," she said.

Ted had told her that the trip had to do with the receipt of a large contribution to aid victims without fault. "I'll be back tonight. Tomorrow, I'll go to Portland and return Thursday evening."

"I know, you told me that."

"Molly, I'm working with some people. I'll tell you all about it when it's over." He knew she assumed it was some kind of a project that he wanted to surprise her with later. She had even helped him load the tools and the plywood panels into his truck. He also knew she would hear about it on the news before his return on Thursday night. There was nothing he could do about that. His plan required secrecy and national television.

"I wish you'd tell me now," she said, turning away.

He couldn't tell her—not yet.

≈≈≈≈≈

Ted returned to the old cabin off State Road 503 five miles east of Ariel. By mid-afternoon he had assembled and installed the plywood panels. A mattress, some blankets, two deep cycle batteries, a hanging light bulb and the two cell phones for incoming calls only were in place. A large cooler had been iced and stocked with food before closing the door and flipping the light off. Nobody would ever find the old cabin. He made his way through the underbrush to his truck and headed west on 503 and then north on Interstate 5 toward Tacoma.

After lunch on Wednesday, the day of the Senator's party, Ted was ready to go to Portland. "I'll be back tomorrow night," he said to Molly while sipping coffee, peering over his cup and looking out at the Sound.

"How large is this contribution?"

"Molly, it's big. I'll tell you all about it when I return."

Molly walked with him to the garage and they kissed tenderly. "You be careful." She placed her hand at the back of his neck to pull him close, cheek to cheek.

"I will," he said holding her warmly.

Ted drove his van south on Interstate 5 to Portland and parked a block away from the Moreland Motel not far from Dayton and Ratcliff Streets—just two blocks from the Federal Bank where the armored truck route terminated. While still in his van he applied make-up to his hands, face and neck to darken his complexion and slipped a wig over his head. He replaced his regular glasses with the black-rimmed glasses, the pair he had bought in New York City. Donning a brown blazer and a forties style felt hat, tilted to one side the way they were frequently worn in old movies, he walked to the Moreland Motel and registered as Bill Smyth from South Bend, Indiana. He paid cash for one night.

In his room, he washed the makeup off. He wouldn't need that again until the Thursday morning, after the Senator's party. He reviewed the ads for old cars in the Portland paper and, using the raspy voice, called six that looked promising and made notes on each one.

# THE HOSTAGES

Ted arrived at the Windoff Country Club at six on the night of the party. He quietly parked his van at the outer fringe of the parking lot. He waited and watched for the arrival of the Senator and his young wife. They parked near the front entrance. In the next hour the parking lot filled. Ted counted three uniformed security guards. Nothing more would happen until the party began to break up. His years in the CIA, and many stakeouts, had taught him to take a break when he could—cool it. Now would be a good time to have dinner. A martini might even be in order. Ted departed the Windoff Country Club.

~~~~~

Two and a half hours later with no moon, the parking lot was dark and secluded. Ted was wearing his dark clothes and no make-up. Three soft felt black hoods, one with eyeholes contoured to fit his face, lay in the seat beside him.

Guests would begin to depart from the country club in another thirty minutes. Ted waited and thought about the voices he would use tonight. D. B. Cooper, of course, would have the raspy voice. Another would have a deep bass voice, very distinguishable, easy to do. The third voice would be high pitched. He might use a fourth voice from time to time—the one he had titled *the Aunt Gertrude voice*.

Sitting in his van, he watched as people began to leave, dignitaries, some of whom Ted recognized. The *paparazzi* snapped pictures. He knew how they anxiously listened for an unguarded remark to create a headline. When a parking slot two spaces away from the Senator's car opened-up, Ted eased his van into it. If people were too close when the Senator and his wife came out he'd have to consider his second plan and follow them to their motel. He hoped that wouldn't be necessary.

The Senator and Marilyn Donovan came out of the building with another couple. Digital cameras fired in rapid succession. Ted was too far away to hear their conversation. They talked for a moment before going in separate directions.

At fifty-six, a large man still sporting a full head of hair, the Senator presented a dashing figure to turn the heads of women and, at election time, the voters. When he spoke, people believed him time and time again.

"The lying bastard—scum of the earth," Ted muttered.

Marilyn Donovan's figure and long blond hair reminded Ted of a joke he once heard: *Every man's dream—to possess a woman who is over-sexed and owns a liquor store.* He smiled. *she doesn't own a liquor store.*

Ted removed his baseball cap and pulled the felt hood with eyeholes down over his head. He replaced his cap. With the other two hoods in his hand, he waited as the Senator and his wife walked toward their car.

≈≈≈≈≈

Tired and anxious to get to their motel, Marilyn Donovan followed two paces behind the Senator. *His friends never talked about the things that interested her. The reception had been too long.* "I hate these parties, everybody's so old."

"Oh, shut up, we're almost to the car—stop grumbling."

*He's a pain in the ass. I wish we had two motel rooms.* "It's dark and I can't see. This black pebbly asphalt is hard to walk on in these heels." She knew that Jay never liked security and he wasn't bashful about telling them to bug off—they saw and reported too many things. The rental car squawked and the interior lights came on when the remote unlocked the doors. She reached for the door and heard a strange man's voice:

"Don't move or you're dead."

His voice was raspy and spoke with authority and no nonsense. A dull pain in her side radiated through her body. It's a gun—she was sure it was a gun.

"Look straight ahead, Mrs. Donovan" the raspy voice said as he jabbed the gun into her side. "You too, Senator."

Jay gasped.

"I'll bury this knife to its hilt, Senator," The threatening voice sang out. "Now lean over, put your hands on the trunk of the car, spread your legs. Do it, Senator. You too, Mrs. Donovan."

The chicken she had eaten for dinner rose in her throat. She stepped forward—leaning—her hands on the car. Swallowing hard, she stared at the ground. Jay parted his feet.

"We'll kill you if you don't do as you're told," another man's voice intoned, harsh and frightening. "Put this hood over your head." He was speaking to Jay.

"What do you want?" Jay said.

"Never mind what we want! Just do as he told you," the raspy voice commanded. "Put that hood on."

A quick glimpse revealed a gloved hand passing the hood to Jay. She tasted the chicken and felt the burn in her throat. Jay raised his arms and pulled the hood down over his head. She swallowed.

"You. . . ." He was talking to her now. "Put your hands back on the car." That raspy voice again.

"Ooh!" The gun jabbed her ribs. "You're hurting me."

"It's going to hurt a lot more if you don't do as we tell you. . . Here, take this. Put it over your head," another voice.

She took the hood, a soft heavy black felt bag with a drawstring and pulled it down over her head.

"Lean against the car, Mrs. Donovan." The bag closed around her neck as he tied the drawstring loosely—total blackness—she swallowed.

"Senator, put your hands behind your back." A third man, or was it a woman? Then she heard clinking metal.

"Now you, Mrs. Donovan, put your hands behind your back." She hesitated, the gun jammed into her ribs.

"Do it, Mrs. Donovan," a much deeper voice.

The cold metal cuffs snapped around her wrists.

"Come with me," that raspy voice again.

The pressure of a man's grip on her upper arm turned her body and forced her away from the car. They didn't walk far, not more than a few paces.

One of the assailants said roughly, "Put her in here. Put the Senator in this seat."

"Step up, Mrs. Donovan. Move," another one said. The grip on her arm tightened. A hand guided her foot. "Watch your head." One of them guided her head before shoving her into a seat.

"Step up, Senator. . . bend over, duck your head," the person with the high-pitched voice demanded—a woman, she was sure it was a woman. "Hand me the belt.", the same one who had cuffed her.

"Here, take it," The base voice again. The seat belt tightened over her shoulder and across her lap.

"Okay, let's go," a man said.

"Where are you taking us?" Jay said. His voice seemed muffled.

"Shut up. I don't want to hear any more out of you."

"Who are you?" Marilyn said. "Why are you doing this?"

A hard firm hand gripped her throat and shoved her head back against the headrest. "You, shut up," the man snapped. Then he was gone—some shuffling—a door slammed—another door. The vehicle lunged forward and gained speed. Her hair was caught under the drawstring.

Her mind raced from one thought to the next: *Jay is in on this! They're going to kill me—just like he killed Pauline. Oh, God, he really did do it and I'm next.* He always had men to do his dirty work. Any hour of the day or night, Jay always knew someone to call. *Why did they cuff Jay? It's part of the act.*

The trip seemed endless and rough. The meal at the club, the cocktails, those cheese puffs and then the wine and finally champagne. *Oh God, what if I get sick?* She swallowed and then swallowed again.

The bile rose in her throat—she couldn't stop it. Her mouth burned as she gagged. Puke soaked the black hood. Warm goop oozed around her neck and the odor stung her nostrils. The blackness—the odor—endless time—she wanted to scream as the stuff trickled under the drawstring and down between her breasts. The road was rough as they traveled. The terrible smell—would it ever end?

"Stop, I'm sick."

"You, shut up back there. We have a ways to go."

She had no way of knowing how far they traveled. *Oh God, please help me.* When they finally stopped, they took her out first.

"*She smells.*" The raspy voice again. "Whew."

"What a mess," another said. "I could smell her from the front seat. Step down, Mrs. Donovan, it's a big step." They guided her foot.

She listened as they took Jay from the vehicle. A man's firm grip held her upper arm. Her heels sank into soft ground. One shoe stuck in the dirt.

"Come on, let's go," he said, dragging her along.

"I can't, the ground's too soft. I lost my shoe."

"Take her other shoe off," one of them said.

"It's muddy!" She said as a man grabbed her ankle and took her shoe.

"Come on, move," another one said.
"I want my shoes."
"You won't need them."
"Let her get her shoes," Jay said.
"You shut up."

*Now I know they are going to rape me. If I cooperate, maybe they won't kill me.* Sticks jabbed her feet as the men hurried her along. Heavy growth whipped past her knees one step after the next. The sickening odor of the wet hood around her neck made the walk seem endless.

They stopped and she heard the click of a latch. They pushed her ahead onto a cold hard floor. Her feet hit something. A firm grip on her arm kept her from falling.

"Step onto the mattress," a man said.

A hand guided her foot.

She felt the touch and then heard the click of the cuffs. Her hands were free. More clinking, *it must be Jay's cuffs.*

"Now, empty your pockets, Senator. I want everything, your wallet, keys, everything including your shoes."

"I want your bracelet and necklace, Mrs. Donovan." It was another man. She felt his hand on the back of her neck.

"Don't touch me."

"Then do as you're told."

She reached back to release the clasp. He yanked the necklace from her hand and shoved her. She fell onto something soft, the feel of a mattress.

"Give me your watch, Senator," another one said. "I need your watch too, Mrs. Donovan."

"No!"

"Take it Art," the base voice said.

"Don't touch me."

"Give me the watch, the bracelet too."

She manipulated the catch to slip the watch over her hand—then the bracelet. One of the men took them.

"Senator, I want your watch," a man repeated.

She heard movement. *Was Jay giving them his watch?*

More shuffling and then, "When they call, tell them my name is D. B. Cooper."

She heard the sound of a door closing, a clicking sound and then no sound at all. She waited.

"I think they're gone," Jay said. Again, they waited. "It's awfully quiet."

She reached behind her neck and released the knot. As the drawstring opened, regurgitated food spilled down over her body. The wet black hood left slime on her face and in her hair as she raised it over her head. She gagged again and wiped matter away with her hands.

A light bulb hanging on a wire provided the only light. Jay stood there looking at her.

"You're a mess."

The room was the size of a walk-in closet—all unpainted new pieces of plywood butted together to form four flat smooth walls and ceiling with lots of screws in straight rows. She was sitting and Jay was standing on a mattress that had been pushed into one corner. His head almost touched the ceiling. A narrow bit of old concrete could be seen on the other two sides of the mattress. Some blankets and sheets were folded and stacked on the mattress.

She grabbed one of the sheets and began wiping her face, neck and body where the slime had fallen into the cleavage under her dress.

An open-sided box with two shelves, also made of new unpainted plywood, sat beside a big cooler next to one wall. Two phones were on top of the plywood box. Jay spotted them too. He went for them and lifted the two phones from their cradles.

"They're cellular phones," he said.

"Look on the wall," she said, pointing.

There, written on the plywood with a black magic marker, were large block letters:

**THESE PHONES WILL NOT MAKE OUTGOING CALLS.**

*ANSWER WHEN THEY RING. WHEN USING THE PHONE LABELED WITH A PHONE NUMBER YOU HAVE SIXTY SECONDS BEFORE IT SHUTS OFF. IN AN HOUR YOU WILL HAVE ANOTHER SIXTY SECONDS.*

*ON THE OTHER PHONE YOU CAN TALK AS LONG AS YOU LIKE. THAT IS THE PHONE I WILL CALL YOU ON.*

*I WANT YOU TO TELL THE PEOPLE WHO CALL TO GIVE ME A CASHIERS CHECK FOR TWENTY-FIVE MILLION DOLLARS MADE OUT TO THE PORTLAND FEDERAL RESERVE BANK PLUS THREE HUNDRED THOUSAND IN CASH—ALL LARGE BILLS.*

*THIS IS THE ONLY WAY YOU WILL EVER GET OUT OF THIS BOX ALIVE.*

*D. B. COOPER*

She opened the cooler. It was full of food with a block of ice at one end. Two plates and two teaspoons were on the top shelf of the open-sided box. Below that, there was more food. When she saw the paper towels she grabbed the roll and tore a long length to begin wiping more slime from her body. The ends of her hair were wet and stinky.

"You smell awful," he said as he stroked the plywood walls to feel the screw heads sunk deep into the smooth surface. "Did you have to get sick?"

"Yeah, I did it on purpose." God, she hated him.

"We've got to get out of here," he said.

Turning, she saw the outline of a door, a saw-cut on the flat plywood surface with no handles. "I need to go," she said looking around. Then she saw the bucket in one corner. Jay saw it too.

"I guess that's it."

"I can't use that thing."

"Good, you won't stink up the place."

"I have to use it." She was thankful when he turned to give her some privacy.

"We need something to use as a tool."

"Maybe there's something in that cooler." She stood and pulled her panties up.

Jay lifted the lid of the cooler and looked into it. "Everything's in small boxes or bags except for the soft drinks in aluminum cans and some plastic bottles of water."

"I'm cold," she said pulling one of the blankets around her.

"I'm cold too. We'll have to lie down and put both blankets on top of us."

"I'm not getting in there with you."

"Then we each have one blanket and you can stand in the corner."

"I don't want you touching me."

# NATIONAL COVERAGE

After putting Jay and Marilyn Donovan in the old log cabin, Ted drove his van to Dayton and Ratcliff Streets and walked two blocks to the Moreland Motel. The clock on the bedside table read 1:10 a.m. He checked his cellular phone to be sure it was on charge—the one he had labeled #1. He reviewed his clipboard, the things he must do today and set the alarm for 3:15. He'd call Karen Dyer at 3:20—6:20 New York time—forty minutes before her show would begin.

~~~~~

At the National Broadcasting Company in New York City the digital clock on Karen Dyer's secretary's desk indicated 6:22 when she answered the phone.

"A Mr. Cooper is on the line," the CBS operator said.

The secretary remembered the call four weeks ago and the office discussions that had followed. She reached for her note pad and punched the record button. "How may I help you, Mr. Cooper?"

"This is D. B. Cooper. I must speak to Karen Dyer."

"She's busy; her show begins in forty minutes. Give me your number and I'll have her call you."

*D.B. Cooper -aftermath-*

"Listen carefully. My name is D. B. Cooper," he repeated. "My men and I have kidnapped Senator Jay Donovan and his wife. I will call you again in five minutes."

She knew that the Senator's unlocked car had been noticed at the Windoff Country Club and that they never reached their motel. It was part of the morning news. "Mr. Cooper, wait—wait a minute."

"No! You tell Miss Dyer, I'll call her in five minutes."

A click ended the call. She hung up and took off on the run toward the set. Karen Dyer was speaking to one of the camera operators. "Karen, I just received an urgent call."

≈≈≈≈≈

Karen and the camera operator turned to face the young woman as she poured out her story. " . . . . . He said he'd call again in five minutes."

"He kidnapped the Senator and asked for me?" Karen Dyer said.

"Yes!"

"And the call just came in?"

"Two . . . three minutes ago."

D. B. Cooper's words, *you'll do it—you won't have a choice*, reverberated through Karen's mind. "Okay, I'm going to my office," she said as she stepped to a wall phone and entered a three-digit number.

Bill Lubsky answered.

"Bill, I have a breaking story."

"I'll be right there."

She looked at her watch and walked briskly, almost running, toward her office. Bill Lubsky, a seasoned journalist nearing retirement and currently the managing editor for the early morning shift, entered just seconds after she scooted in behind her desk. The cuffs of his shirt were rolled up and his tie was loose around his neck. He sat down in one of the three chairs in front of her desk.

"What's up?" he said.

"A man called and said he's D. B. Cooper and that he kidnapped Senator Donovan and his wife. The switchboard received the call just minutes ago—he asked for me—said he'd call back in five minutes."

"The same man who called you before?"

"Who knows?"

The phone rang. Karen heard the secretary. "Miss Dyer's office." And then the intercom, "Mr. Cooper's on the line."

Karen nodded to Bill. He picked up an extension phone on the small table at the end of a couch. She punched the record button. "Mr. Cooper, this is Karen Dyer."

"Miss Dyer, I'm one of the men who kidnapped the Senator and his wife. You can call them on this number."

She jotted the number on her calendar.

"It's a cellular phone. You won't have much time because the phone is programmed to terminate all calls after sixty seconds. After one hour you can talk to the Senator again. Call as many times as you like but you'll always have that limitation. After you do that, go to the bus station and look in locker 102. You don't have the key so you'll have to break in, or use some kind of a master key. You'll find a cellular phone. I'll use that phone to call you after you leave your office."

She pecked her pencil on the note pad and stared across her desk at Bill Lubsky. "What do you want, Mr. Cooper?"

"I'll call you again on this phone after your show. You will have talked to the Senator by then."

"Where are you?"

"In Portland."

"Portland, Oregon?"

"Yes."

"You know I'll call the authorities."

*D.B. Cooper -aftermath-*

"I assumed you would announce it on your show this morning. That's why I called you at this hour."

She leaned forward clamping her pencil between her fingers with her eyes fixed on Bill. "You want me to put this on national television?"

"Yes, I'll be listening for you to do it. The Senator's life depends on it."

"The western version won't come on for three hours."

"I know that but it'll be on the news as a breaking story within minutes after you announce it."

"Are you the D. B. Cooper who called me four weeks ago?"

"Yes."

"Why did you call me?"

"I need the facilities and talent that you control. Call the Senator. Pick up that cell phone. I'll call you again. Then I'll see you in Portland . . . Good-bye."

Karen sat there clamping the phone to her ear. Then, slowly, she placed the instrument in the cradle. "He doesn't care who we call."

"That's what he said."

"I'm going to call the Senator now." She laid the pencil aside and glanced at the scratch pad to see the number.

"Aren't you going to call the FBI first?"

She picked up the phone. "There are a lot of people to call. We've got twenty-eight minutes and I want confirmation." She punched in the Senator's number and started the recorder. The phone rang. "Pick up the phone, Bill!"

"Hello," a man's voice—loud and excited.

"This is Karen Dyer in New York. Is this Senator Jay Donovan?"

"YES."

She moved the phone away from her ear. "Where are you?"

"In a box . . . WE CAN'T GET OUT!"

"Where."

"I don't know! You called us! Is this one of your damn publicity stunts?"

*It is the Senator, no mistaking that.*

"Tell them to get us out of here," a woman's voice.

"Who's that?"

"My wife, we're in this box and we can't get out. Cut the shenanigans and get us out of here."

"How did you get there?"

"We were kidnapped by three or four men. They brought us here with hoods over our heads. Now get us out of here."

Karen held her pencil not believing what she was hearing. "Can you tell me anything that'll help us find you?"

"He said his name's D. B. Cooper."

"Let me have that phone," his wife screamed . . . "YOU'VE GOT TO GET US OUT OF HERE."

Again, Karen moved the phone away from her ear and listened as the woman sobbed.

Then, the Senator, "You have to get . . ."

The signal cut-off. "Hello, are you there?" The phone was dead. Slowly, Karen returned the phone to its cradle. "What do you think of that?"

"I don't know."

"We need to pick up that cell phone."

"I'll take care of that, you need to be on the set."

"It's a scoop. My first announcement will be brief. We need to pull the file on D. B. Cooper. Call the FBI, tell them everything and that I'm going to Portland." She thought of Mike, the managing editor for the CBS New York office, her boss and he just happened to be her husband. "Maybe Mike'll go with me."

"You couldn't stop him from going."

She smiled. "He's my favorite, Bill."

"I would never have guessed," Bill Lubsky said with a grin.

# They're Desperate

Senator Jay Donovan was standing just inches away from his wife when he put the phone down.

She turned to the wall crying. "You've got to get me out of here."

"With no tools, what do you expect me to do?" *She is so dumb.*

"You should have kept your knife; you always have a pocket knife."

"They took it, you know that." *Karen Dyer is up to something. She is always nosing around.*

"You should have figured out a way to keep it. How long have we been here?"

"How do I know? Ten, twelve hours maybe."

"When they call again, ask them what time it is."

She wrapped the blanket tighter around herself and laid down on the mattress. As he knelt down on the mattress with the other blanket around his body he smelled her vomit. The phone rang—he bolted off the mattress. "Hello," he yelled clutching the phone in his hand. A second ring sounded.

"It's the other phone," she said.

He snapped the flap closed and grabbed the other phone. "HELLO!"

"This is D. B. Cooper."

"Get us out of here."

"I will, as soon as you give me a cashier's check for twenty-five million dollars made out to the Portland Federal Reserve Bank plus three hundred thousand in cash—all large bills. Your instructions are written on the wall."

The Senator looked at the printing on the wall. "I don't have twenty-five million dollars." He looked down at his wife. She was sitting with the blanket wrapped around her.

"Senator, you steal that much every year. That's what it's going to take to get you out of that box. When they call, you'll have sixty seconds. Make the most of it. Has Karen Dyer called you yet?"

"She wouldn't tell me anything."

"I'm the only one who knows and I won't tell until you pay up."

"How'd she call us?"

"I gave her the number."

"She'll tell the world about you and we'll never get out." *That damned woman.*

"Yeah, she'll do that. Just get the money."

"Ask him what time it is!" Marilyn said. She stared up at him with the blanket tight around her body.

*Damn, how she smells.*

"Sounds like she's losing it," Cooper said.

"She wants to know what time it is."

"I'm not telling you anything until I get that money. Bye bye."

The connection ended.

"What time did he say?" Tears rolled down her cheeks.

"He wouldn't tell me."

≈≈≈≈

The countdown had started. Karen shifted papers. She was seated behind a console, her lapel mike in place, the earpiece concealed under ringlets of auburn hair fluffed comfortably over a sky blue jacket with a white blouse. The teleprompters were on although she wouldn't use them for her opening remarks--all that had changed—5—4—3—2—1:

"Good morning ladies and gentlemen, welcome to NEWDAY on this Thursday morning, November 15th. We have a breaking story to report. Senator Jay Donovan and his wife have been abducted. Just minutes ago I spoke with the Senator. Senator Jay Donovan confirmed that three or four men abducted him and his wife last night. They are entrapped in some kind of an enclosure in the vicinity of Portland, Oregon. The abductor claims to be D. B. Cooper, the man who jumped out of an airliner in 1971 after stealing two hundred thousand dollars. He called CBS and gave me the phone number to call the Senator. As the story unfolds, we'll have more to report."

She disconnected herself and stepped off the set as the news segment started. Bill Lubsky was waiting.

"I just talked to Mike and told him what happened. He wants you to go to Portland as soon as possible."

"What about the cellular phone?" She asked.

"The FBI is picking it up."

"We need to alert the authorities in Portland too."

"The FBI will do that. Mike is trying to reach Biff now."

"Good." She liked Biff Roberts. As a cub reporter fresh out of school, she first met him twelve years ago. His area of supervision included all of New York state and part of New Jersey with the title of Area Supervisor in the FBI, a position he had held for ten years. Prior to those duties, he was with the San Francisco Police Department twenty-one years, the last two as Chief. With a slim physique and jet black hair he looked younger than his fifty years.

≈≈≈≈≈

Biff Roberts was at home when he received the call from his office. "Mike Dyer called a few minutes ago. He said a D. B.

Cooper had phoned Karen Dyer and told her that he kidnapped Senator Donovan and his wife last night."

"D. B. Cooper?"

"Yes, Karen Dyer has already talked to the Senator."

"She has a phone number to talk to the Senator?"

"That's right. Mike Dyer gave me the number. He said we could only talk for a minute, then the line cuts off."

"Did you try calling the Senator?"

"No, I called you. Mr. Dyer said it would be an hour before we can call the Senator again."

"Have you notified Bowers?" Steve Bowers was the Director of the FBI. His office is in the J. Edgar Hoover Building in Washington DC.

"I've got a call in for him now. His wife said he was out jogging."

Jogging, with his weight, that must be a sight to behold, Biff thought. "Tell her to find him."

"I did."

"You better notify the President."

"Before I talk to the chief?"

"Yes. I'll be there in twenty minutes."

~~~~~

Steve Bowers was alone in the men's room just two doors down the hall from his office. The buttons on his vest fit snugly around his belly as he pulled and pushed each button through the mating hole. He didn't like being short and heavy. "I'm just built that way," he told himself and others.

It had been almost forty minutes since his wife informed him of the call and he'd sped to his office. Biff had briefed him. Rinsing his hands and then reaching for a paper towel, he muttered, "Damn…why does Donovan always have to be the limelight?" There are too many things pending, too many lids to blow off—and Karen Dyer. "We sure don't need that bitch nosing around."

Bowers left the men's room and turned toward his office. Biff had explained that a call to the Senator could be made at seven-thirty. It would be a conference call with Biff in New York City and Bowers in Washington DC. The recorder was ready.

At seven-thirty, Biff called. "I'm going to place that call now, Chief."

Bowers hit the record button. "Good." He waited, not more than a few seconds.

"He's on Chief," Biff said.

"Hello!"

It was the Senator. "Jay, this is Steve."

"Steve, get us out of here."

"We don't know where you are."

"What do you mean? You're calling me."

"Jay, we have no way to trace it."

"Don't tell me that. They track every call."

"The cellular phone has a New York area code. We know you are not far from Portland but there's no way to pinpoint your location. We don't have much time. Tell me, how did you get there?"

"They brought us in a van I think. Call Karen Dyer; she's in on it; get her. She knows."

"She knows where you are?" Bowers fiddled with his pencil and pressed the phone tight to his ear.

"Yeah, she called me here—her and then this Cooper guy."

Jay's right, Bowers thought. She's in on it. Mike Dyer's the one who called Biff.

"They put hoods over our heads."

"How long a trip was it?"

"Long time, an hour or more. Marilyn puked all over herself."

"Can't you peg it closer than that?"

"Steve, we couldn't see anything and they want me to give them twenty-five million dollars."

"Twenty-five million?" Bowers scribbled *25 mil* on his pad.

"They want a cashier's check for the twenty-five million made out to the Portland Federal Reserve Bank plus three hundred thousand in large bills."

"He'll never be able to spend them and we'll stop payment on the check." Bowers wrote *$300,000—large bills* on his pad.

"That's what he said, all large bills. Call Roger and tell him to give Cooper the money."

Roger Stark was the Senator's attorney.

"How do we give the money to him?"

"Hell, I don't know, do something. Get us out of this box. Make Karen Dyer tell you."

"How many were there?"

"Three or four." The Senator was shouting now. "The bastard called a while ago right after Dyer called. Tell Roger to give them the money."

"Ask him what time it is," a woman's voice.

"Is that your wife?"

"Yes, she wants to know what time it is."

"How's she doing?"

"She's hurting, we both are. Call Roger and tell him to get that money."

"Okay, I'll . . ." The signal ended.

"The call lasted exactly sixty seconds, Chief," Biff said.

"Biff, you think Karen Dyer's in on this?"

"No, of course not." Biff said. "She's covering the story."

"She's always probing around."

"She's a journalist and she's good at it."

"Right. I'll call Roger and get things started on this end. We'll call the Senator again in an hour. Talk to you later."

*Roger is always in his office early when he's in town, before any of his staff.* Bowers punched the intercom. "Sonya, get Roger Stark on the phone." *Karen Dyer, I wish I could do something about her.*

"Mr. Stark is on the line," Sonya reported.

"Roger, we need to talk one-on-one away from the office. Can you meet me right now?"

"Donovan?"

"Yeah, he and his wife have been kidnapped and Karen Dyer is in the middle of it."

"I know. I heard the news. We do need to talk. See you in ten minutes."

The grounds of the Federal Triangle was a short five-minute walk midway between their offices and a frequent meeting place for private conversations with Roger.

# The Conspiracy

At 7:45 on this brisk November morning, the grounds of the Federal Triangle were deserted—a good place to be inconspicuous. Roger Stark stood near a park bench—a portly man. His appearance made Bowers think of Winston Churchill every time they met.

"You think Karen Dyer's in on this thing?" Bowers said with no salutation as he approached.

"She has a lot of contacts," Stark said.

"She called Donovan first. It may be a ploy to get at him, or us. She's good at that. We gotta stop her one way or the other."

"We have to find out what she knows," Stark said.

"She's going to Portland. Biff said there's some kind of a special phone that he is picking up."

"We're out of control. You're going to Portland, aren't you?"

"I wasn't planning on it. I told Biff to get a charter for himself and two agents out of the New York Field office."

"Why don't you take your plane and pick'em up in New York? Tell Roberts to invite Karen Dyer to ride along with you."

"All right, I'll do that. I think you should call Dave Lewiski."

"What are you thinking about?" Roger Stark said.

Dave Lewiski and Carol Fleming ran the operation in Washington and Oregon for Rostel Barstelli. Carol Fleming's accounting firm delivered a large amount of cash to Stark by courier every quarter, most always driving through, to be distributed to special people in Washington D. C., money that did not appear on any books. Bowers knew that Barstelli would like to get his hands on Karen Dyer. "This might be a good time to quiet Karen Dyer once and for all."

"I'll call him."

"Roger, when I call the Senator again I think you should listen in on it. We can only talk once each hour for sixty seconds."

"What do you mean?"

"Cooper's got it rigged."

"Clever little bastard, isn't he?" Stark said.

"He sure is. I'll call you just before I call Donovan and we'll make it a three-way conversation."

Ted Bolan sat in his motel room in Portland at four-thirty on Thursday morning. The cell phone he had used to talk with the senior Senator and Karen Dyer, lay on the table. Yesterday's newspaper was on the bed opened to the want ads—*Used Car Sales.* He had called on four of the ads yesterday afternoon, before the Senator's party.

The television played softly. CNN had just reported that a man identifying himself as D. B. Cooper had abducted Senator Jay Donovan and his wife. They transmitted a portion of Karen Dyer's announcement. She had scooped everybody.

"Here's to you, Karen Dyer." Ted raised his empty coffee mug.

*Gene Elmore*

Marilyn Donovan was lying on the mattress with her blanket wrapped around her when Jay lay down beside her. She moved as far to her side as she could. "Don't touch me."

"You little bitch. It's time for you to learn a little respect." He threw the covers back. She sat up and scooted off the mattress cowering in the corner, her legs folded and tucked under her. He grabbed her hair. She screamed. He slapped her hard and pushed her onto the mattress. Straddling her body he pinned her down and slapped her again—one, two, three times.

"Get off me!" She clawed at his face.

He hit her again with a closed fist, held her arms and then allowed the weight of his body to cover her. She screamed.

"I don't want to hear another word from you. You're my wife and I'll take you anytime I want." He rolled off her.

She sprang to her feet massaging the bruise on her face. Oh how she hated him. Somebody had told her that you could hit a person on the side of the head at the temple and knock them unconscious for two, three—five minutes, maybe longer. *Something hard, the bucket, something in the cooler maybe?* She lifted the lid and looked down into it. The aluminum cans, *a can of soda might do it.*

She needed something strong. She had seen it on TV—her pantyhose maybe. She saw the cords going to the two cell phones. They were plugged into a receptacle that looked like a cigarette lighter, the kind she had seen in cars. She turned. He was lying on the mattress, half covered. *He liked root beer.* She hesitated—thinking—hurting. She had hated him for so long.

Turning toward him, she said, "I'm sorry I got angry. I should not have fought with you that way. I'm sorry."

He turned and stared at her.

"Would you like a root beer?"

Lifting his head—his eyes wide open, looking at her—hesitating, "Yes."

She got a root beer and a coke out of the cooler. He sat up as she handed the can to him. He opened it.

"Don't you want me to open yours?"

"No, not yet." She knelt down on the mattress beside him sitting on her heels. "I'm really sorry for the way I acted. You're right. I should be more loving. Why don't you let me give you a rub down the way I used to right after we were married?"

She saw his eyes. *I know he's stripped every girl in his office, or is he down to one now, the way it had been with me before we were married? It was only a matter of time until he'd kill her—another accident, like his first wife. Pauline didn't drown in that pool. He threw her in after he killed her. The doctor's report had confirmed that.*

"You're not mad at me?" he said taking his first sip.

"No, it's been such a long time. Roll over on your stomach." She leaned down to kiss him. "Take your coat off."

He sat his drink on the floor beside the mattress and removed his blazer before rolling over on his stomach with his arms at his sides. She straddled him and began to massage his neck and shoulders. She knew how he liked it. "Close your eyes honey . . . relax."

She rubbed his neck and shoulders and took his head gently in her hands to turn it. "Rest easy honey, relax." She stared at the spot where she needed to hit him—his temple. She could feel his breathing under the weight of her body. His eyes were closed. She reached for the full can of Coke. Her hand wrapped tightly around the can, almost crushing it. The blow was swift and hard. He moved. With both hands she hit him again and again and again. He lay still.

She sprang to the cabinet and pulled the wire from one of the cell phones and yanked the other end from the receptacle at the wall. Moving fast she was on top of him again. She passed the wire three times around his neck, knowing that each turn would increase the pressure. It wasn't long enough for a fourth time around. Using both hands she pulled it tight. The wire sank into the furls of his neck. The veins above the tourniquet swelled and the skin reddened. He stirred and she pulled it tighter. He gasped and she held on until he wasn't moving anymore.

Slowly she eased off. *I'm rid of the lying, cheating bastard.*

# The Plan Takes Shape

Steve Bowers called Biff and told him to include Roger Stark's office on the next call to the Senator. "Since Roger is the one to arrange the money, we need to keep him in the loop. Also, cancel that charter, I'm going to Portland. I'll pick you up at eleven in New York."

Then he called the airport and arranged for the FBI plane to take him and the New York contingency to Portland. "Plan on a ten o'clock departure with one stop in New York."

At 8:35 Biff called. "Roger Stark is on the line and we're ready to place that call to the Senator," Biff said.

Bowers waited for the click of the phone indicating that Biff had completed the connection.

"HELLO!" Her voice was ear splitting.

It was Marilyn Donovan.

"Mrs. Donovan?" Bowers said.

"Get me out of here!"

"Mrs. Donovan, let me talk to the Senator."

"You've got to get me out of here!"

"Let me talk to the Senator!"

"He's sick. He can't come to the phone."

"Mrs. Donovan, I must talk to the Senator."

"He can't come to the phone. What time is it?"

"Where are you?"

"I'm in a room made of plywood. Why don't you come and get me?"

"Mrs. Donovan, the Senator said Cooper wants twenty-five million."

"Call Roger, tell him to give him the money."

"Roger's on the line."

"Hello, Marilyn," Stark said. "Put the Senator on."

"Roger, give him the money. Get me out of here."

"Marilyn, let me talk to Jay."

"I told you, he can't come to the phone. What time is it?"

"What's wrong with him?" Stark said.

"He's sick. You surely know where I am."

"No we do . . ."

The call terminated.

"The signal lasted sixty seconds, Chief," Biff said.

"Biff, I want to invite Karen Dyer to ride with us."

"She may have some staff and equipment."

"That's okay, encourage her to come with us."

≈≈≈≈≈

The morning sun reflected through the floor to ceiling glass panes in the CBS conference room that overlooked the New York skyline, illuminating the polished walnut surface of a table large enough to seat twenty people. With her hand resting on a notepad, Karen twiddled with her pencil. *Why did Cooper select me? It is fun being a part of it. We'll scoop everybody.*

The operator at the CBS switchboard had been advised to ring the conference room instead of Karen's office. Mike and four executives were sitting around the huge table waiting for Cooper's call. He said he'd call after the NEWDAY show ended. They all had a phone and the recorder was near her hand ready to go. At nine thirty-five, the phone rang. She punched the record button and they all picked up their phones. "This is Karen Dyer."

"Good morning Miss. Dyer. The Senator told me you called."

"They're desperate." Her eyes swept the room. The four executives were leaning forward clamping the phones to their ears.

"I know. They're in a plywood box," Cooper said.

"How many of you are there?"

"There are other things we need to talk about. I asked the Senator for three hundred thousand in large bills and a cashier's check for twenty-five million dollars made out to the Federal Reserve Bank to help fund victims who are without fault and, more specifically, those at the World Trade Center. After the check and the money have been delivered to me, I'll tell you where the Donovans are."

"They'll stop payment on the check and you'll never be able to spend the money."

"No they won't stop payment and the money will spend just fine. Find out who Donovan's attorney is. Tell him what I just told you. You might also tell him that we'll have no problem killing the Senator and his wife. It'll be over in a matter of minutes if he doesn't follow instructions. I want that check and the $300,000 ready for delivery this afternoon. I'll call you in Portland on the cell phone from locker 102 about four-thirty Pacific Standard Time to tell you when and where to deliver the check and the money. Give me your cell phone number, as a backup, just in case there's a problem.

Karen thought about that for a few seconds before giving him the number.

He repeated the number and then ended the call by saying, "all communication will be through you—talk to you later."

Karen was stunned. She wished she had thought to ask about the FBI position. They'll never stand still for a journalist handling all communication.

Mike broke the silence. "Isn't that a strange twist? Use Donovan's money to fund the victims. He'll be furious."

"What do we do now?" one executive asked.

"Karen and I are going to Portland," Mike said.

Karen smiled as she once again remembered Cooper's words four weeks ago: *You'll do it—you won't have a choice.*

~~~~~

Molly rolled out of bed a few minutes before seven. She missed Ted and never liked sleeping alone. Ted said he'd be back tonight. She clicked the TV on and turned the volume up a bit so she could hear the news in the bathroom. The western version of the NEWDAY show would start in two minutes. Tossing her gown, she stepped into the shower.

With the shower running and soap all over her body she could only hear bits and pieces of Karen Dyer's opening monologue. She heard the words, *D. B. Cooper*, hit the shut-off valve and grabbed a towel. Moving into the bedroom, she listened the last few words of Karen Dyer's opening remarks.

In the lower right corner of the screen Molly noted the time . . . 7 a.m. Eastern Standard Time—*three hours ago.* "Maybe I didn't hear D. B. Cooper, another Cooper no doubt," she said under her breath. She gathered the towel around her body and stood silently as she watched the live west coast version of the news.

Molly thought of Ted. I wonder if Ted knows about this. She went to phone and punched in his cell phone number. It rang three times before Ted answered.

"Hello Molly."

"Have you seen the news? D. B. Cooper has kidnapped Senator Donovan and his wife."

"Yes, I saw it."

"What do think?"

"Molly, I don't know what to think. I'm in Portland taking care of that foundation contribution. I'll be home this evening."

# ANOTHER CONSPIRACY

Rick Marchak sat in the bar and poolroom in Portland, Oregon. He owned the place. His breakfast plate was empty and the large mug had just been refilled with hot coffee. He stared over the empty tables. A television above the bar was playing and the news had just ended.

Ricardo Angelli, Marchak's partner, slipped into the other side of the booth.

The waitress approached with a mug and coffee pot. "What would you like? Mr. Angelli." She filled the mug and sat it down on the table.

"Scramble them easy, Sarah."

She scurried away.

Rick Marchak and Ricardo Angelli were distributors working for a man they knew only as Rostel Barstelli—a man they had never met—a man they had only seen on television when Karen Dyer had interviewed him. He had good stuff and delivered on time, a man you didn't cross.

Following the Karen Dyer interview a warrant had been issued for his arrest and he fled to his villa in South America. Several of his men were awaiting trial. His east coast connections had been virtually eliminated.

Business in Washington and Oregon was conducted through Dave Lewiski.

"Have you seen the news this morning?" Rick Marchak said, speaking to Angelli.

"The D. B. Cooper thing?"

"Yeah. Karen Dyer is coming to Portland. Dave Lewiski called. Barstelli wants her picked up—alive if possible—kill her if we have to."

"Hey . . . it ain't worth the risk. She's not on that drug campaign anymore."

"That's what I told Lewiski. He said Barstelli would pay $35,000 if we take her alive, five on delivery and thirty after she's out of the country. If we kill her we get twenty."

"She's a celebrity. It's not like grabbing some doll off the street."

"Ricardo, she hurt us bad with that damn campaign. Four guys are in prison and a lot of stuff will come out at the trial. Two of them will probably get death."

"Barstelli must want her real bad."

"Yeah, she's a real beauty. That's what sucked him into that frigging interview. She trapped him into saying some things he should not have said." Marchak said as he plucked a cigarette from the pack. The flame flared out of his old Zippo.

"You're going to burn the whole place down with that thing."

"I like it," Marchak said, dragging deep and reaching for his cup. Smoke drifted out through his nostrils—a nose that was too large for his face. He wished it was smaller. "If Barstelli'll buy her, I'd like that better than killing her. They'd really take care of her!"

"Baestelli laid off after she ended the drug campaign because of the risk and not wanting any more notoriety. We have to find a way to grab her with nobody seeing."

Sarah sat Angelli's food on the table and topped off both coffee cups. He reached for the salt and pepper.

Marchak sat back in his seat, coffee in one hand—his cigarette in the other. He envied Angelli's good looks and his

*D.B. Cooper -aftermath-*

way with the women. *He always has two or three on the string.* "You aren't messing around with anyone now are you?"

Angelli laughed. "Huh . . . No but I won't pass up an opportunity to take on Dyer if I have a chance." He held a bite of egg on his fork. "All hell's going to break loose when she disappears. We'll have to grab her with no trace."

"Come on, finish your breakfast, let's call Lewiski and tell him we'll do it."

≈≈≈≈≈

Marchak's office was a messy small niche in the back of the bar and poolroom. He placed a call to Dave Lewiski, a stocky man, forty years old with jet-black hair. Marchak knew that Barstelli and Lewiski were close, like brothers.

"Call me when you have her," Lewiski said.

As Marchak hung up he reached for a cigarette and stared at Angelli. "We need to make plans."

"Yeah, I guess we do."

"Let's go on stand-by starting at three at your place with four men and one car. You and I can drive my Ford Ranger with the camper shell."

"What are you thinking about?" Angelli said.

"We'll have to watch and wait for an opportunity. Get some rope, duct tape, a body bag, chloroform and some small towels and anything else you can think of?"

"I'll bring some cuffs. That should do it."

"Okay, your place at three o'clock."

Angelli slipped out and closed the door.

*Barstelli'll kill her when he gets his hands on her and it won't be quick.* Marchak tilted back in his chair, smiling at first and then more solemn. Profits are down and sales are more risky. Barstelli should not have consented to that interview— Karen Dyer's questions had him squirming. *I hope he makes her hurt bad.*

When Dave Lewiski called Barstelli and told him that Marchak would do the job, Barstelli's response was quick and right to the point.

"Pick me up in Astoria about three this afternoon." Astoria, Oregon was the nearest airport to accommodate Barstelli's jet. "We'll drop in on Carol unannounced."

"Where are you now?"

"In Mexico City. It has been six months since I've been in the states. It'll be safe enough. There are some things we can go over and I want that bitch. If Marchak takes her alive, I can whip her out of the country in my jet."

Somewhat surprised at his boss's quick decision, Lewiski said, "You won't have any trouble with clearances?"

"No, I talked to my pilot after you called. Things have loosened up to get the planes back in the air. They won't be looking for me and he knows all the tricks."

"I'll pick you up at three." He wondered if Barstelli was doing the right thing. Rostel Barstelli began seeing a lot of Carol Fleming ten years ago after her father died and she assumed control of his accounting firm. She was twenty-eight then, Barselli was thirty-six. Her home sits a hundred feet back from the Columbia River—a half-mile wide at that point—a natural lake fifty miles northwest of Portland at Cathlamet, Washington. The grounds encompassed thirty-two acres all the way to State Road 4, a thousand feet away from the house. She and Barstelli had lived together until that warrant was issued for his arrest.

Carol Fleming didn't like South America and the time between her visits became longer. Barstelli hadn't seen her for four months. Lewiski was sure she was running around. "We haven't caught her with anybody but she's gone much of the time. She has a sixth sense, or somebody's tipping her off."

# THE PLAN MOVES AHEAD

Following breakfast, Ted picked up the paper on the bed in his motel room and reviewed the circled ads he had called yesterday. He called one of the numbers. The car had sold. Another ad stated:

> 1981 Ford, four-door, runs good, needs some body work, must sell, $300.

Ted entered the phone number and looked at his clipboard to see the name he had used. A man answered. Ted was sure it was the same man who answered before. "Good morning, Mr. Wright. This is Leonard Gibbons. Do you still have the eighty-one Ford?"

"Yeah, I still have it."

"I'd like to see it. I can be there in a couple of hours."

"I'll be here."

Ted hung up and called a second number. Someone answered on the third ring. "Al's Wrecking Yard."

Checking his clipboard, he said, "This is Naylor Pearson. I was talking to Jake yesterday about an old Chevy wagon."

"This is Jake. Like I told you yesterday, it's not much, a piece of junk."

"You said it runs good."

"Yeah, it even has some good rubber but the body's shot, rusted out. It needs everything."

"You said I could have it for a hundred and a half."
"Yeah, that's more than I can get out of it for salvage."
"I'll be there before noon."
"Okay."

Before leaving his motel room Ted applied makeup to his face and hands to take on the appearance of a man with a deep suntan, a Hispanic look. He slipped the wig in place. A baseball cap shaded his eyes.

He drove his van to the casino parking lot in La Center, thirty miles north of Portland and parked. He grabbed his empty briefcase before locking the van and walked to the bus stop to catch a bus back to Portland. In Portland he boarded a local bus to go to the address Mr. Wright had given him to see the old Ford. The car was dark green faded with a lot of rust. The tires weren't much but they would do. He drove it around the block. It seemed to run okay. Wright wanted $300 for it.

"I'll give you two hundred dollars for it." He pulled the cash from his pocket.

"Is that the best you'll do?"

"That's it, take it or leave it."

"I'll take it."

Wright signed and dated the title. Ted gave him the money. He stopped at the first gas station and put in five gallons. He drove the Ford to Dayton Street, parked a block away from Ratcliff Street and left the empty briefcase in the old Ford.

He caught a bus to the wrecking yard. Jake was right, the old station wagon was decrepit. "You say it drives okay?"

"Drive it if you want to. Like I said, it's a piece of junk."

"I'll take it around the block."

"Fine."

It didn't run too bad. The gas gauge didn't work. After paying Jake the $150 and picking up the signed title, he stopped at the first gas station and put in ten gallons. From there he went north on Interstate 5 to the casino parking lot in La Center and parked next to his van. He took Old Granny, the life-sized dummy he had made, out of his van, propped her up in the front seat of the old station wagon and fastened the belt around her big belly. He tossed the bib overalls, a shirt, old shoes, a straw hat and the Rufus ID in the back seat.

He headed north out of La Center in the old station wagon, turned onto a two lane county road and drove one mile to a point where the road curved sharply under a heavy growth of trees—the same place he had checked out two weeks ago. He turned into the obscure opening grown over with tall weeds and brush that was just wide enough for two cars. The old Chevy wagon was virtually invisible fifty feet off the road with enough space to park a second car beside it.

Ted looked at his watch. His timing was okay. He made his way out of the brush and hiked to the corner a mile away to catch the bus to Portland.

In Portland a local bus transported him to the corner of Dayton and Ratcliff. A park provided a place where he could see the intersection. He saw a neighborhood tavern across the street. It would be another six hours before the armored truck would go by.

He walked the two blocks to the Federal Bank where the armored truck would end its route and saw nothing out of the ordinary. He moseyed back to the corner and then into the neighborhood tavern. A television was playing with the volume turned down. He took a booth in one corner and ordered a sandwich and a beer. *This will be a good place to stay out of sight when all the commotion starts.*

He walked to his motel. Check out time was 1 p.m. He'd lounge around the park or sit in the old Ford for a couple hours after that. He checked his makeup. The black-rimmed glasses were in his pocket. It might be a good idea to give the Senator another call. Ted entered the number for the unrestricted phone. It rang five—six—times before he heard her voice—soft and meek.

"Hello."

"Has the Senator arranged for the money yet?"

"Yes! Why don't you let me out of here?"

"I will, Mrs. Donovan, as soon as I have the money. Let me speak with the Senator."

"He can't come to the phone," she said somewhat louder than before.

"Why, what's going on?"

"He's just sick, that's all. What time is it?"

"I have to speak to the Senator, Mrs. Donovan."

"Can't you understand he's just laying there not moving. Get me out of here."

"I'll get you out as soon as I can, Mrs. Donovan." He closed the flap. Something is wrong. The Senator would never have let her do the talking.

# On to Portland

KOSI was a television station in Portland, an affiliate of CBS. Mike called and made arrangements for them to meet the plane. "There will be six of us and some equipment," he said. "We're flying in the FBI plane arriving in Portland at one-thirty your time."

Shortly after takeoff, Bowers told Mike and Karen that Mrs. Donovan answered the second time he called. "The Senator was sick, she was hysterical—a screaming maniac. Tell me Mrs. Dyer, why did Cooper call you?"

"I have no idea. Maybe he's a nut and has the hots for me. You should see some of the letters I receive."

"Cooper said he wanted to communicate through Karen," Mike said. "She needs that phone from locker 102."

"We can handle this now. It would be better if the media backed off while we negotiate," Bowers said.

After landing at the Portland International Airport, as they were loading into a KOSI van and car, Biff came over to Karen and Mike. "Bowers still wants to keep the media out of this."

"We're going to cover this story, Biff and we won't be far away," Karen said.

"Yeah, I know."

"Bowers is a personal friend of the Senator," Mike said.

On the take from the Senator would be a better way of putting it, Karen thought. Barstelli all but implicated him and the Senator. *I was so close to getting them.*

"He likes to throw his weight around," Biff said.

Mike laughed. "You don't sound like you like him very much."

"Damn it Mike, I'm not saying anything you haven't heard before."

"Don't worry about it Biff," Karen said. "He and the Senator are two of a kind."

"You're right there," Biff said. "They deserve each other. It makes you wonder how the system works at all."

"We'll be at KOSI," Mike said.

~~~~~

Steve Bowers had commandeered a conference room at the FBI Portland field office for his command post. The cellular phone from locker 102 lay on the conference table with a microphone attached for a recorder and two extension phones. The clock on the wall indicated four forty-two, twelve minutes past the time when D. B. Cooper said he'd call. The phone rang.

Biff Roberts and another agent picked up extension phones.

"Hello," Bowers said. He hunkered over the table, pencil in hand.

"Who is this?"

"This is Steve Bowers, Director of the FBI."

"Where's Karen Dyer?"

"She's not here . . . who are you?"

"I'm D. B. Cooper and I want to know where Karen Dyer is."

"We don't need her." He leaned forward a bit more, pressing the phone tight against his ear.

"Is she in Portland?"

"Yes."

"Does she have the check?"

"I have the check."

"Bowers, I never liked you and I don't like talking second-hand, so please hear me well. You tell Karen Dyer to be at the corner of Dayton and Ratcliff Streets with her staff of photographers in one hour. If you value the Senator's life she'd better be the one who answers this phone when I call."

"We don't need Karen Dyer," Bowers said.

"Like I said, she better be the one."

The connection broke. Bowers closed the flap to end the call and looked around the room. Biff had turned away. "Call Karen Dyer, Biff. Tell her to be at Dayton and Ratcliff Streets in one hour."

"You want me to take that phone to her?" Biff said, facing his Chief now.

"Yeah, do that but tell her I want to be in all the calls."

≈≈≈≈≈

The KOSI van and several police cars were parked in the vicinity of Dayton and Ratcliff Streets. People were gathering. Mike, Karen and all of the staff awaited Cooper's call.

The weather had been unusually warm for a fall day in Portland. The temperature was falling and just passing through seventy with the sun setting low in the west at four-thirty in the afternoon. The camera was ready to focus on Karen. She was still wearing the sky blue jacket with a white blouse and a skirt. She had considered changing to sandals but decided to stay with heels. The night air would be cold. She tossed a three-quarter-length coat over the seat.

The phone rang right on schedule. A technician punched the recorder that had been rigged to the cell phone as she answered. Mike and Bowers each had an extension.

"This is Karen Dyer."

"I hoped you would answer. Do you have the check and the $300,000 in large bills?"

"Bowers has them."

"Okay, tell him to have it ready."

"Bowers is listening."

"Good, when I call the next time, be sure we're on camera live so my men can watch. Is your equipment ready to roll?"

"Cooper, what are you leading up to?"

Miss, Dyer, I'll kill the Senator and his wife. Now, is your equipment ready to roll?

"Yes."

"Are you transmitting live now?"

"No, we're recording."

"Get Chief Oran Biskbey on one of the phones," Cooper said.

"I don't know Oran Biskbey."

"He's the Chief of Police in Portland and he's standing about fifty feet from you."

"He's over there," Bowers said, pointing.

"Get him over here," she said.

"Get Biskbey," Bowers yelled to an agent standing nearby.

Karen saw him walking briskly toward the van in a tailored uniform with a side arm on his right hip—about fifty years old, six feet and wearing thin-rimmed aviation style glasses. *Nice looking man.* "He's coming."

"I assume you've rigged extension phones," Cooper said.

"Yes, two."

Mike handed Oran Biskbey his extension phone.

"We're both on the line," she said. "Mr. Bowers, The Director of the FBI is on the other extension."

"Good—in about thirty minutes I'll call and instruct you to drive to a designated location. After arriving, how quickly can you transmit live on national television if you make preparations for it now?"

"From Portland?"

"Just two blocks from where you are now."

"Two . . . three minutes. It'll be recorded so we can broadcast it later."

"No, I want a live transmission. I told you that. Get some helicopter coverage."

"You want helicopter coverage?"

"Miss Dyer, I want all the coverage you can give me. Like I said, my men are watching. If they can't see what's going on, they'll know exactly what to do. The Senator's life depends on it. Do whatever you have to do to get ready. Can you do it with one van?"

"Yes."

"Chief Biskbey, I see a lot of police cars. You may want some yellow tape ready to cordon off an area. After the live transmission begins, one of your cameramen must be able to move about outside of the van to stay with you."

"How far from the van?" Karen said.

"Can you go a hundred feet into a building?"

"Yes."

"That's far enough. Later, you and Chief Biskbey will follow me with whatever back-up you want."

"You're giving a lot of orders, Cooper," Oran Biskbey said.

"Hey, it's your call. All I want is TV coverage. If that stops, the Donovans die."

Bowers stepped over to Karen. "Give me that mike." Karen handed it to him. "This is an FBI matter, Cooper. Chief Biskbey and Karen Dyer have no authority here."

"I don't know why the Director of the FBI would even be here. I don't like you or the Senator, so butt out. I want all the officers to be in uniform under the direct command of Chief Biskbey. I'll call you in thirty minutes." The connection ended.

"Well, I guess we have our work cut out for us," Karen said, speaking to Biskbey. "I'm Karen Dyer."

"I know who you are, nice to see you in person."

"What does he want you to do?" Mike said.

She explained. Turning to Bowers, she asked, "you do have the money with you?"

"In that brown envelope." Bowers said, pointing to one of his men.

"I'll call and clear the way to start broadcasting in thirty minutes." Mike said.

"Let's go on the air right now," Karen said.

"Good idea."

"I don't want you to do that," Bowers said. "Hold everything until I approve it."

"It's a breaking story," Mike said, "and we're going to run with it."

Karen reached for the lapel mike and earpiece stored in a compartment in the van, clipped it to her collar and laced the wire under her blouse. She plugged the wire into a small transceiver, clipped it to the waistband of her skirt and flipped the switch. "Am I transmitting?" She looked at one of the techs.

"Loud and clear, Miss. Dyer."

# THE ACTION BEGINS

Ted Bolan sat in the corner booth in the tavern and watched the camera pan around to show all the activity and then focus on Karen Dyer as she presented her live report. He slipped out of the booth and stepped outside. A few people had gathered around the front entrance of the tavern watching the police cars and the KOSI van 300 feet away. He watched and waited. Karen Dyer stood near the van with her photographer.

Chief Biskbey moved about among the staffers and police officers. Two police cars had pulled in behind the van. The minutes passed and then he saw it. The armored car was coming down Ratcliff Street. It made a left at Dayton. He stepped away from the people with his cell phone in hand to punch in the number for the phone from locker 102.

~~~~~

When the phone rang Karen Dyer looked at the tech and then at her watch—four fifty-two—twenty-eight minutes since Cooper's last call. The sun was just above the horizon and she felt the chill in the air. The tech punched the record button as she answered. "This is Karen Dyer."

"Is Chief Biskbey on the line?"

"Yes."

"I see you've started your live coverage."

"Yes."

"There is a Federal Bank on Second Street. Make an immediate left turn from where you're parked and go one block. Park your van at the curb within twenty feet of the front door."

"We'll lose our signal while the van is moving," Karen said.

"How about the helicopters?"

"They'll be watching."

"I see two."

"One is the KOSI copter. The other one is from another station."

"How long will you be off the air?"

"A minute or so."

"Good. My men are watching so be sure your roving cameraman is ready to cover everything live. After you park I will join you and we'll go into the bank together with the camera running. Chief, have one of your officers alert the bank personnel as to what we are doing."

"What are we doing?" Karen asked.

"We are going to make a bank deposit. You may want to cordon off the area and clear everybody out."

"You're giving a lot orders," Chief Biskbey said.

"Hey, like I said, it's your call, my men are watching, the Senator is sick so we need to end this situation as soon as possible." The phone clicked and the line was dead.

"Let's go," Karen said.

≈≈≈≈≈

Rick Marchak, Ricardo Angelli and the six men watched the television as she reported the live action. "They're going to the Federal Bank building, let's go," Marchak said.

≈≈≈≈≈

Molly had watched every news broadcast since that first one early this morning.

# NATIONAL COVERAGE

The move to the bank did not take long. The van and two police cars were near the front entrance.

Karen checked the lapel mike and small transceiver to be sure the wire under her blouse did not show. She slipped her three-quarter-length coat on and pushed the earpiece into her ear. She also had a wireless hand mike. "Testing, one, two, three, four."

"Loud and clear, Miss Dyer," one of the technicians said. "How do you hear me?"

"Loud and clear. Pipe us through now."

The camera focused on her. She saw the technician's finger rise and start counting—3—2—1.

"Ladies and gentlemen you are witnessing a crime in action. As we have reported all day, D. B. Cooper and his men are holding Senator Jay Donovan and his wife hostage. We are in front of the Federal Bank building in Portland. A man who claims to be D. B. Cooper directed us to come to this location and wait. He hijacked an airliner in 1971. They never found . . ."

As she spoke a crowd gathered. Two officers stood guard while six others pushed people back and began stretching yellow tape fifty feet away.

"This man from the past has requested national coverage," Karen continued. The camera panned. She saw the last of the yellow tape go in place to mark a restricted area. The stage was set. She was having fun doing something that she did well, being this close to the action, a reminder of her years as an overseas correspondent. She saw Mike standing off to the side smiling. Hosting the NEWDAY SHOW did have its rewards, being home most every night and all but live action is more fun.

People watched from their position beyond the yellow ribbon. She saw an old dark green car approaching and watched an officer block its path. The officer turned and yelled, "He says he's D. B. Cooper."

"Keep him covered and let him through," Biskbey said.

The officer lifted the yellow ribbon to let him pass under while two officers, one on each side, walked along. The old Ford stopped a few feet from the KOSI van. The driver got out walking erect with the gait of a young man. He carried a briefcase. A black hood covered his face with a baseball cap pushed back on his head. He stepped past the van to where Karen was standing.

If he's the real D. B. Cooper, he'd have to be in his seventies, she thought. He wore an old jacket, dark trousers and gloves. Karen extended the hand mike toward him.

"Hello Miss Dyer. Are we on live television?"

The same voice she heard on the phone—raspy. The black hood had the shape of a face with eyeholes fitting close over a pair of glasses with large lenses. "Yes," she said.

He turned toward the woman holding the camera. "Where are the other cameras?"

"This one and the cameras in the helicopter are the only ones active now."

"And that one is transmitting now?" he said, gesturing toward the woman holding the camera.

"Yes," Karen said. "I have the mike in my hand and a lapel mike."

"Good . . . hold the mike so everyone can hear me. Are they transmitting from both helicopters?"

"I don't know about the other copter but KOSI is transmitting and recording from this camera," she gestured toward the camera operator, "and the camera they have on board the copter. The studio may switch to the helicopter from time to time. I assume the other helicopter is transmitting and monitoring our frequency."

"But you can talk to both of them?"

"They're hearing everything."

"Good. Let me see the check."

Bowers stepped forward slipping the check from his coat pocket. He handed it to Cooper. To Karen it seemed that Bowers was anxious to get rid of it.

Cooper looked at the check. "Where's the money?"

"We have it," Bowers said. "It's in that brown envelope." He pointed to the officer holding it.

"You have all the serial numbers properly recorded?" Cooper said.

Bowers looked at Karen and then back at Cooper, before answering. "Yes, of course."

"Good, give me the money."

Bowers nodded and the officer handed a brown envelope to Cooper.

"Okay, let's go in, you, Chief Biskbey, the lady with the camera and the FBI Director."

"I want two of my officers," Biskbey said.

"That's okay," Cooper said. He turned and led the way into the bank.

The bank manager was waiting in the middle of the lobby.

"I want three hundred thousand dollars, all twenties," Cooper said.

"We don't keep that kind of money on hand," the manager said.

"Don't lie to me. You just had an armored truck pull in with some large cash deposits. Most of it is probably already banded and counted. Now get some of those bags in here now. I want to see you count it out."

The manager hesitated. "Tell him to do it Chief," Cooper said, turning to Biskbey.

"You've got to do it. He's holding Senator Donovan and his wife hostage."

"Yes, I know," the manager said.

"Then you know what has to be done," Biskbey said. "Get the money in here and start counting."

"It's in the counting room where the armored trucks enter the building," the manager said.

"Take us back there," Cooper said.

The manager looked at Biskbey.

"You have to do it."

"Quit stalling," Cooper said.

The manager led the way through a door. The room was large with open steel trusses above and two overhead doors to accommodate vehicles. Many of the bags had already been removed from the truck and were sitting on tables. The woman with the camera moved in behind Biskbey and the manager. Karen saw the men in uniform from the armored truck reaching for their guns.

"Keep your guns holstered," Biskbey called with his hands out in front, his fingers spread wide. "He has hostages."

The three guards from the armored truck and three people from the bank, two men and a woman, were in the room as Biskbey and the manager led the way.

"Use that table to count the money," Cooper said pointing to an empty table.

"We need to count out three hundred thousand dollars, all twenties," the manger said to the guards.

"Now, this is what I want," Cooper said speaking into the mike that Karen held but loud enough for all to hear. "Keep that camera focused on that table as they count. Turning to the bank manager, Karen followed him with the mike, "Keep track of how much you take out of each bag. Write it down."

The manager and the three people started counting and writing figures on a yellow pad as they took money from one bag and then another—all twenties just as he said. Cooper was right. Most of the money had already been banded.

"Keep the dialogue going, Miss Dyer. I want the world and my men to know exactly what we are doing."

"What you see, ladies and gentlemen is a crime in process. The officers of the bank are counting out money as we stand by, helpless to stop it."

The camera woman turned to pick up a shot of Karen Dyer as she talked. "D. B. Cooper and his men, are holding Senator Donovan and his wife hostage as we watch, threatening to kill them if his instructions are not followed."

"Okay, we have the money counted, three hundred thousand, all twenties in neat stacks," the bank manager reported. The camera turned and zoomed in to view the money.

Karen looked at her watch. *The counting had taken no more than two, maybe three minutes.*

Cooper opened the briefcase he had carried in from the old Ford and removed a white envelope before handing the briefcase to the manager. "Put the money in this," Cooper said.

The manager placed the money in the briefcase.

Cooper closed the case and handed the manager the brown envelope that Bowers had given him. "There's three hundred thousand dollars here, a gift from your dear Senator. It'll replace all the money you just counted out."

Karen couldn't help smiling when she saw Bowers, his mouth dropping open. *So much for an easy trace of the large bills.* They didn't have a single serial number. She wished Biff and Mike had been here to see it.

"Keep the camera on the manager and me," Miss Dyer. Then, addressing the manager, Cooper said, "I have a cashier's check for twenty-five million dollars made out to a Federal Reserve Bank. The account numbers and the bank information for the World Trade Center Relief Fund are in this envelope." He held up the white envelope he had just taken from his briefcase. "I want you to deposit this check to that account."

"I don't know if I can do that," the manager said. "The banks are closing."

"Don't fuss with me. You can do it. That bank won't close for another thirty minutes." Then, turning to Chief Biskbey, "Tell him."

"You have to do it. Let's get this over with."

The group made their way back into the bank with the manager. As Karen moved into the lobby she saw the manager hand the check and the paper he had taken from the white envelope to a girl behind the counter.

"Get up here Miss Dyer," Cooper called. "Make sure everybody sees and hears all of this." Then, turning to the manager, "tell her again."

The camera focused on the girl, Cooper and the manager while Karen extended the mike for all to hear.

"Deposit this money to the account shown here." The manager said gesturing to the open envelope and paper in her hand.

"Watch her do it," Cooper said to the camerawoman as the girl slipped into her chair at her computer.

"A cashier's check for twenty-five million dollars is being deposited to the World Trade Center Relief Fund," Karen said to the TV audience as the camera focused on the girl at her computer.

The nimble fingers of the teller made entries in the computer and then hit the print key. "The money has been deposited, Mr. Keller," she said to the bank manager. She stepped to the printer and handed him the print-out.

"Our business is finished," Cooper said, taking the print-out and leading the way to the street. Turning to Karen and speaking into the microphone, "Miss Dyer, I had to devise a way to insure that Senator Donovan's money would go to victims who are without fault. The World Trade Center victims are good examples. There are many victims just as deserving that may not have been in the World Trade Center on September 11th.

"We all know that Senator Donovan stole that money," Cooper continued, "and it's time to expose him for what he is. The $300,000 is a side issue between the Senator and me for all the trouble he created—all those dishonest things he did."

Cooper turned to Chief Biskbey but still speaking into the mike, "Chief, you and Miss Dyer follow me if you like. I assume those helicopters will track me. My men are watching and they know what to do if things don't go well."

Cooper turned and walked to the old Ford with his briefcase in hand. The engine started and he maneuvered toward the yellow ribbon.

Karen and Chief Biskbey had to hurry. "I'll drive," Biskbey said, sliding in behind the wheel. Two officers jumped in back. Four more ran toward another car. Karen passed the wireless hand mike to the technician as she slipped into the front seat.

"What about the van, Miss Dyer?" the woman with the camera shouted.

"Stay here," Karen called as she slammed the door.

Whipping the car around, Biskbey turned toward the yellow ribbon. Officers held the yellow tape for them to pass under as both police cars followed the old green Ford. Karen pulled the earpiece out of ear and let the short wire dangle under her hair.

≈≈≈≈≈

Marchak and his men were standing around the Ford Ranger watching.

"What do we do now?" one of the men said.

"The TV van isn't moving and that's her husband. Sit tight," Marchak said. "We'll go wherever he goes."

# The Escape

Cooper didn't seem to be in a hurry, Karen thought as he made his way from one light to the next and then onto Interstate-5 north. She glanced back, one police car with four officers followed. "What do you think he's going to do?"

"We'll be crossing into Washington soon." Biskbey took his cell phone from his belt and punched in a number. "Washington is out of my jurisdiction. I'm calling Grant Taylor, the sheriff of Clark County."

"I used to know a Grant Taylor—went to high school with him," Karen said.

Then, speaking into his cell phone, Bisksbey said, "Grant, Karen Dyer and I are following this Cooper guy going north on Interstate 5. We'll be passing into Washington shortly." .... "Fine, we'll keep in touch." Biskbey closed the flap to end the call. Then, speaking to Karen, "He grew up in Seattle, about your age, short but tough as nails, you'd like him."

"That's just the way I remember him," she said. Then, peering through the windshield, she added. "Isn't there something more we should be doing?"

"Cooper's ordered everything I would have requested, Helicopters—everything. When I learned that you were going to Dayton and Ratcliff Streets I ordered a police copter. Cooper doesn't know about that."

"Ha . . . I wouldn't be too sure he doesn't know and I don't think he'd care anyway."

"You may be right. It'll be dark soon."

"He probably planned that too. I bet he gets away," Karen said.

"How?"

"You know he has a plan."

Biskbey smiled. "If I were betting, I think I'd bet on him."

Twenty miles into Washington, Karen asked, "Do you think he's the one who jumped thirty years ago?"

"I believe it. I was here when he did it. There's a celebration in Ariel every Thanksgiving—all kinds of memorabilia."

"I know about that," Karen said. "I was raised in Seattle and Dad took all us kids to one of the annual events. I must have been about ten at the time. I bet we all go this year."

"You have to. You're one of the stars now."

"It does seem that he has taken a liking to me—he said he met me once. I think he knows you too. He knew to ask for you."

"If he lives around Portland he would know me as the chief."

"I'll bet he has met you. The Ariel exit is coming up."

"It's two exits ahead off to the right of the freeway on 503 ten miles east . . . he's exiting toward La Center unless he goes west toward the Columbia River."

Biskbey followed on the two-lane road past some houses into La Center. Karen looked back to see if the police car was following. It was.

"There's La Center's claim to fame. You may have heard of it?" Biskbey said, pointing.

"The hardware store full of manikins?"

"Then you have heard of it?"

"Yes."

They followed Cooper through La Center and then north another half mile. Cooper made a right turn onto a county road and drove another half mile before stopping. Getting out, he walked back to the two police cars.

Biskbey, Karen and the officers in the other car opened their doors as Cooper approached.

Karen got out and stood near the right front fender of the patrol car. The others joined Biskbey on the left. Cooper stood near the front bumper facing them. The knitted hood shrouded his face with the baseball cap pulled down shading his eyes. The whirling of the two helicopters five hundred feet above made it difficult to hear.

"Chief, stay here to block this road. Cordon it off. Don't let any more cars come through."

"You've got your money," Biskbey said. "We need to know where the Senator is."

"I'll call you. Do you have the cellular phone?"

"It's back at the van," Karen said.

"That's the one I'll call you on."

"What about cars coming out?" one of the officers said.

"I don't care what you do. Let'em go, get'em out of the way. All I want is for one of those helicopters to watch you to be sure you don't follow me. Stay put for about twenty minutes and then do whatever you like." He turned and walked briskly back to his old Ford. Then, before he entered the old Ford, he shouted, "I'll call you on that cell phone."

Biskbey ran to his car and grabbed the mike and switched to channel B. "Jason, this is Biskbey. How do you read? Over." He released the mike button.

"Loud and clear, Chief."

"You were watching everything?"

"Yeah but all we're hearing is the KOSI chopper reporting the chase. The KATI chopper is transmitting on another channel and we're listening to that too. What's going on down there?"

"Cooper just left in the old green Ford. Follow it."

"You still want us to stay out of sight?"

"I don't care what you do—don't lose him."

"Looks like the KATI chopper is already breaking away to follow him," Jason said.

Karen was beside him. "What are you doing?"

"I just instructed my police helicopter to stay with him."

"May I have the mike?"

"If you want your chopper, go to the other car. This mike is on channel B."

She moved quickly to the other car to call the KOSI chopper. She learned that the chopper had been broadcasting continuously reporting the chase. She asked to be piped through. "Ladies and gentlemen you are watching the chase of a man identifying himself as D. B. Cooper. He just instructed Chief Oran Biskbey to stop here and wait for twenty minutes and not let anymore cars pass. You just saw Cooper leave in the old Ford. Stay tuned for continuous coverage."

She returned to Biskbey. He was talking to the police copter. "I want you to watch the old Turner Road."

"We're on him Chief. We'll get him. Wish we had infrared. It's hard to see in all those trees."

"I know, do what you can. Maybe you'll see headlights."

"Will do."

"Where is he?" Karen asked.

"The tree line starts on down this road about another half mile. The only outlet is the Old Turner Road. It's a shortcut to the freeway. It's kind of rough but he may try to use it."

Karen stepped over to the other car and the officer handed her the mike. "KOSI One, this is Karen Dyer. Pipe me through to the TV audience again."

"Okay, you're on."

"Ladies and gentlemen, this is Karen Dyer. What you are seeing and hearing is a live transmission of a crime in progress. D. B. Cooper just drove away in an old car and the pictures you are seeing are being transmitted from the KOSI helicopter. As you saw, he just disappeared into the trees under the cover of darkness. At this time I'm going to transfer the audio to the helicopter where the reporter can describe the live action as he watches."

Karen returned to Biskbey at the other car. "What do you think Cooper's going to do?" she said

"JC Four reported that he's driving without headlights and the trees are dense. It's like looking for a speck in a jar of lard.

"Here comes a car," Karen said. She was looking where they last saw an old Ford. The KOSI helicopter flooded the area with light. Even so, the glare of the headlights blinded them. A light-colored sedan approached. Biskbey and two other officers blocked its way as it eased to a stop. A man and woman were in the front seat with a medium size dog between them. Biskbey approached the driver's side and asked to see a driver's license.

"Where you heading?" Biskbey said.

"To the Columbia River, my brother has a cabin there. What's the problem?"

"We're looking for an escaped fugitive. Would you mind stepping out for a moment, both of you. . . open your trunk?"

They got out and Biskbey walked around the front of the car and noted the license number on his pad and then moved around the right side to the trunk.

Karen followed the man toward the rear of the car. He opened the trunk. It had a couple sleeping bags and other miscellaneous items. Biskbey leaned in and thumped the floor and squatted with one hand on the pavement to look under the car. Karen turned when she heard a second car approaching—an old battered station wagon—a hundred years old, she thought. It rolled to an easy stop a few feet behind the first car.

"Did you meet another car?" Biskbey asked the driver of the first car.

"When?"

"Before we stopped you."

"No."

"You sure? It was an old dark green Ford."

"I don't remember one. It's pitch black in those trees."

The woman stood quietly beside the car with her head forward looking at the pavement.

"You surely would have seen the headlights if a car was going the other direction," Biskbey said. "I don't see how you could have missed seeing it."

The man didn't answer.

"Okay, you can go," Biskbey said as he turned to approach the second car.

Karen watched the man close his trunk and return to his car. The woman got in. As they drove away Karen followed the chief. "Where you heading?" she heard him say before asking for identification.

The driver appeared to be an old man. "To La Center, the hardware store. Dewey is waiting for me," he said.

"I need to see your driver's license."

He extended his wallet for Biskbey to see.

"Take it out," Biskbey said. The old man complied and handed him the ID.

"What's that?" Biskbey said, looking through the car window and pointing.

"That's Old Granny. I'm taking it to the hardware store in La Center. It's for Dewey."

To Karen, looking through the windshield, the old lady looked almost real.

Biskbey wrote something on his pad, returned the ID and peered through the open front window, with his flashlight in hand before continuing down the left side of the old station wagon. Karen could see the illuminated area from Biskbey's light as she moved along the right side.

"Would you mind getting out and opening the back?" Biskbey said.

"Naw, I guess not." The old man in bib overalls got out and moseyed back to open the tailgate. His bib overalls were tattered and his shoes were old and dirty. His straw hat was frayed around the rim. The flooring that covered the sunken compartment in the old wagon was rusted through—empty except for an old wheel with no tire.

Biskbey's light flashed across the old man's face. Hispanic, Karen thought.

"Did you meet another car before we stopped you?" Biskbey asked.

"Just one."

"Where?"

"A ways down the road."

"What color was it?"

"Dark, no headlights."

"Okay, go on." Biskbey said.

The driver returned to the old station wagon and closed the door. As he pulled away, Biskbey turned to Karen. "I wonder why the first car never saw anybody."

Karen ignored the question. "Did you know the man in the old station wagon?"

"I know of him, Rufus, he's been around for years. Makes manikins."

"Is there a road where Cooper could have turned off?" Karen asked.

"No, I don't think so. He may have pulled off the road when he saw the on coming car. I don't really know this area that well. The Old Turner Road is at least a couple miles as I remember." Biskbey picked up the hand held radio. "JC Four, can you see anything up there."

"It's getting pretty dark Chief and we haven't seen anything on the Old Turner Road."

"How far is the Old Turner Road?" Biskbey asked.

"It's a good five miles from where you are to the turnoff and he won't be able to move very fast after he turns. That road's awful. Nobody uses it anymore."

*D.B. Cooper -aftermath-*

"I didn't know it was that far. Keep watching it." Biskbey released the mike button and looked at his watch before turning to Karen. "Come on, let's go."

"It hasn't been ten minutes yet."

"I'll have the other patrol car stand by. Let's drive on down that road into those trees and see what we can see."

She jumped in the car as Biskbey slammed his door and hit the starter. "I better tell the copter what we're doing."

Biskbey handed her the mike and flipped back to the normal police channel.

"KOSI One, this is Karen Dyer, over."

"Go ahead, Miss Dyer."

"Chief Biskbey and I are going to drive on down the road to see what we can find. Can you stand by and watch this area for a few minutes?"

"We can do that."

Going five miles to the Old Turner Road—they saw nothing. Biskbey pulled to the side of the road and turned around. "I'm going to get things started," he said taking his cellular phone from the clip on his belt and punching a pre-programmed number.

"Who are you calling?" Karen asked.

"I'm calling Grant Taylor. He knows this area a lot better than I do."

She watched as Biskbey clamped the phone tight to his ear.

"Grant, this is Oran."

"Yeah" Karen heard Biskbey say. "We need to cover this road from one end to the other." ........ "Great, I'll be watching for you. Miss Dyer and I will head back to the intersection." He punched the button to end the call. "He's going to send two men out to watch this road for the next couple hours."

"It sure gets black out here."

"Yes it does and there's no moon."

"We may as well go back to the KOSI van," Karen said.

"Yeah, we'll leave two officers here until Grant and his men arrive. He's hiding in there someplace and you need to get to that phone. Cooper said he'd call."

"I agree. May I use your phone?" Karen said.

"Sure."

She punched in Mike's cellular number. He answered on the second ring.

"Honey, Chief Biskbey and I are coming back. He's turning everything over to Sheriff Grant Taylor because he knows the area and has jurisdiction here. Cooper said he'd call to tell us where the Donovans are."

"I've been listening for that phone to ring. The KOSI van hasn't moved and the forensic team is still working. I'll wait for you here. Maybe we can squeeze in dinner, just the two of us."

"I'd like that. See you soon."

≈≈≈≈≈

Ted Bolan turned into the casino parking lot in La Center and parked the old Chevy wagon beside his van. After tossing old Granny, the black hood, dark clothes and his briefcase into his van, he used 409 on the steering wheel and door handles of the old wagon. He would have liked to have washed the make-up off his face and hands and removed the bib overhauls but that would have to wait. For now he wanted to move out as quick.

# ALL HELL BREAKS LOOSE

As Karen and Biskbey approached the bank only two police cars remained. The KOSI van had not moved. The yellow ribbon was gone and people were moving about normally. She was anxious to have dinner alone with Mike. He was standing near the van. She opened the car door and stepped out as Biskbey eased to a stop.

"I'll be at the station for the next thirty minutes," Biskbey said. "After that they can reach me at home if you need anything."

"I'll call if I need anything," she said as he drove away. The, turning to Mike, "I'm ready for that dinner."

"Me too, I'm so glad to have you back."

"I need a restroom. I hope there's one close?"

"I just came from that Chevron station." He pointed across the parking lot to a row of businesses on the other side of the street. "The men's room was clean and the ladies room is right beside it. You have to see the attendant for the key."

She started and then turned back. Her coat flared open at the front. "I need to get the phone." She stepped to the open door of the van and reached inside to take the phone from its charging cord and checked to be sure that it was on before slipping it into the side pocket of her skirt.

The KOSI crew was packing things away. "We'll be here a few more minutes, Miss Dyer," one of the techs said.

She felt the small transceiver with the tiny wire strung under her blouse. I need to get unwired, she thought. That'll have to wait.

"I'll see you shortly," she said starting across the parking lot with a fast gait.

"Okay, Honey."

Mike had a look in his eyes that said, 'Hurry back.'

≈≈≈≈≈

Marchak leaned forward gazing through the windshield. "Where's she going?"

"We'll soon find out," Angelli said.

They watched Karen Dyer walk briskly across the well-lighted Wal-Mart parking area toward the Chevron station on the far side of the street.

"Hell, she's going to the john," Marchak said as he opened his door. "Come over here," he called to the men in the other cars.

Marchak, Angelli and the six men gathered in front of the Ford Ranger.

"I think she's going to that Chevron station. Angelli and I will circle around through the alley with the Ranger and pull up behind the station to wait for her to come out. Nolan, you handle the rag. Give her a good dose. The rest of you stay ready. If somebody comes, stop them. Find a reason. No rough stuff, we want her to simply disappear. After it's over, I'll drive around the corner and wait for you to follow me."

"Maybe we should take her inside the can," one of the men said.

"Somebody might see us jimmying the lock. Take her when she comes out."

≈≈≈≈≈

Karen entered the Chevron station and asked for the key.

"It's hanging on the wall." The attendant pointed. "It's the one with the pink paddle."

She sensed his excitement.

"You're Karen Dyer?"

"Yes."

He had a nice smile, nice-looking young man with a wedding band on his third finger.

"The ladies room is around the corner past the men's room."

A light between the restrooms illuminated the area at the side of the station. Mike was right; the restroom was clean and well maintained. She opened the door and slipped into one arm of her coat as she stepped out and turned. She saw the flash of a hand reaching from behind. Her head reeled back held in a vise grip of a man's arm across her throat. A cloth covered her face and burned her eyes as she sucked a deep breath to scream. Her arms were pinioned and the awareness of a violent struggle gave way to lethargy.

≈≈≈≈≈

Marchak, Angelli and Nolan with the chloroform, held her until she stopped struggling and slumped in their arms.

"Go open the tailgate, Nolan. Spread the bag out," Marchak said. "Grab her legs, Angelli."

Nolan tossed the open bottle of chloroform and rag as he ran to the Ford Ranger. He lifted the rear door of the camper shell, dropped the tailgate and opened the canvas bag to spread it out.

The slim figure of Karen Dyer sagged between the two men as they carried and placed her on the open bag.

"Get that coat out of the way," Marchak said.

Nolan and Angelli yanked the coat from her and tossed it into the Ranger. They tugged at the fabric of the bag to encase her body as Marchak closed the long zipper. They pushed her into the truck, slammed the tailgate and dropped the rear door of the camper shell.

"You drive," Marchak said to Angelli. "Nolan, tell the others that it's over. We'll wait for you around the corner."

As they turned the corner, Marchak punched a number into his cellular phone. It rang three times.

"Who's calling?"

"This is Marchak. We got her."

"Anybody see you?"

"No, they don't even know she's missing."

"How many of you are there?"

"Angelli, me and six others in three cars."

"Get rid of them. You and Angelli go north on 5 to the Rose Valley, exit 16. It's forty miles from Portland. Go east one mile, you know the place, it's that old house I've owned for years that we have used before, been boarded up for the last six months. I'll be waiting at the garage with the doors open. You'll see the headlights of my car. What are you driving?"

"A gray Ford Ranger pickup with a camper shell."

"Okay, see you there."

≈≈≈≈

Opening her eyes to total blackness, Karen was vaguely aware of her surroundings. She was in a moving vehicle lying on a hard surface with her arms close at her sides. When she tried to roll over she felt a sharp pain at her side and closed her fingers around the small transceiver clipped to the waistband of her skirt. The gradual recall of the intense struggle, the chloroform—obscure at first—and then. "OH NO," she screamed, kicking and clawing at the abrasive fabric.

The jostling slowed. The vehicle stopped. She listened but heard nothing except the engine. They were moving again, not far this time. Doors opened and closed. Men's voices, what were they saying? Doors opened again—slammed, moving, turning, gaining speed.

The coarse material in which she was encapsulated provided a scant cushion between her body and the hard surface. Her arms were confined, restricted by the close fitting canvas. A bag—a body bag—*oh God, please help me.*

# THE BODY BAG

Ted was in his van driving north to Tacoma. He was anxious to see Molly. *By now she would have heard the news. How was she taking it? Should I call her or wait? He'd be home in an hour.* He could tell the authorities where the Donovans are now. He'd call Molly after he talked with Karen Dyer. He must remember to use his own phone to call Molly and the one he purchased in New York to call Karen Dyer. After that he could destroy the New York phone and D. B. Cooper would be at rest. He entered the number for the phone from locker 102 and pressed SEND.

≈≈≈≈≈

The sound of the phone was barely audible over the rumbling of the moving vehicle. She had forgotten that. *I couldn't have called out anyway.* The abrasive texture of the course material scuffed her hands as she fumbled to find the pocket. Her skirt and slip had gathered around her waist. It rang again, a third time. *Oh, please don't hang-up.* Now, she had the phone in her hand but it was caught in the pocket as it rang a fourth time. Using both hands she freed the phone and fumbled for the cap "Hello!"

"Hello, Miss. Dyer."

That raspy voice. "Why are you doing this to me?" The phone was clamped tight against her ear in total blackness.

"Stop shouting. I'm calling to tell you where to find the Senator. . . ."

"You bastard, I believed you."

"Why are you so angry?"

"You have me trapped in this bag. What kind of ransom are you holding me for you sick bastard?" She squirmed and the small transceiver dug into her side.

"I don't know what you're talking about. Where are you?"

"Damn you, get me out of here."

"I don't know anything about your situation."

She slammed the lid closed, arched her body and kicked. The heel of her shoe caught and held her leg in a cramped position. *The clever SOB sounded so convincing.* "What have I done." She clutched the phone in one hand and clawed at the fabric with the other. The violence within her gave way to crying, total horrible blackness. The phone rang. She lifted the flap and pressed it to her ear—crying—incoherent.

"Miss Dyer, I want to help you."

She cried—she couldn't speak.

"You sound like you're in terrible trouble."

"I . . . I am."

"Can you tell me about it?"

"I'm in a bag in a moving vehicle."

"What do you mean, a bag?"

"A bag! A body bag! I can't see anything!"

"What happened?"

"They slapped a rag over my face. When I woke I was in this bag. I can't see anything. She pushed the material off her face.

"Where did this happen?"

"At the Chevron station across from the bank."

"You were alone?"

"Yes . . . Mike was across the street at the KOSI van." She sensed the slowing of the vehicle—the turning. "They're stopping!"

"Miss Dyer, I have to think. I'll call you."

"No, no, don't leave me."

"I have to work something out. I'll call you soon. I promise."

The call ended. "No no, don't go."

≈≈≈≈≈

Ted Bolan pulled off the freeway at the next exit and slowed to a stop. He had watched her for so many years applauding the way she moved about on the set—that auburn hair falling loosely to her shoulders—her trademark—a beautiful lady. He didn't know Biskbey's number. He picked up the phone, entered 911 and pressed SEND.

A man answered the call on the first ring. "How may I help you?"

"This is D. B. Cooper and I want to talk with Chief Biskbey in Portland."

"The D. B. Coo . . . "

"Yes and I want Chief Biskbey."

"Give me your location."

"Never mind my location. Senator Donovan's survival depends on you doing the right thing. Get Biskbey, or give me a number where I can call him, NOW!"

"I'll put you on hold."

"Don't you put me on hold. YOU keep me on the line while you do whatever you have to do."

"Yes, Mr. Cooper."

Ted reached for his clipboard and checked his pencil to be ready to copy. Seconds passed. "What are you doing that's taking so long?"

"We're trying to find Chief Biskbey's number." It was a woman.

"Who are you?"

"I'm the supervisor on this shift."

"Can't you pull it up on the computer?"

"It's an Oregon number. We have to look it up. I'll patch you through as soon as we find it."

The wait seemed endless.

"I'm patching you through."

The phone rang three times. "Portland Police."

"This is D. B. Cooper. I need to speak with Chief Biskbey."

"Ju. . .just a moment."

Ted's edginess—the image of Karen Dyer in a bag created a stiff intolerance within his body—he'd have to be careful about making mistakes. "Calm down," he told himself. *How had things gone so badly? What happened?*

"Cooper, this is Biskbey."

"I had to call you on 911 and I'm sure everyone is listening. Give me a number to call you direct."

"Where are you?"

"Never mind where I am, give me a number."

Biskbey rattled off a number and Ted noted it on his clipboard reading it back as he wrote.

"That's right," Biskbey said.

"Make sure it's not busy." He hung up and then entered the number. It answered immediately.

"This is Biskbey."

"Chief, what happened to Karen Dyer?"

"What are you talking about?"

"Don't you know?"

"She's with her husband at the van."

"When I called to tell her where to find the Donovans she was trapped in some kind of a bag."

"Cooper, what are you up to?"

"She's in trouble. I just found out about it when I called her."

"Where is she?"

"I don't know where she is."

"How'd you call her?"

"Chief, I called her on that phone I gave her. I don't know what I can do but I think it would be safer and in her best interest, if you make sure everybody is off this line."

"Why should I believe you?"

"Because Karen Dyer's in trouble."

"I think you need to tell us what you know and tell us where the Senator is now."

"Chief, I'm going to say this one time and you will have the choice of being hostile or cooperating. I'm not about to tell you where the Senator and his wife are until Miss Dyer is free. I had nothing to do with her abduction."

"You've proved that you are a clever bastard, Cooper and we can't trust you. Not only are the Donovans missing but now you are telling me that Karen Dyer is missing. Next, you'll tell us how much these abductors want and where to deliver it. No no, you tell us where the Donovans are and then we will have a reason to believe you. Right now, I'm sick of you."

"I'm the only link you have and I'd like to communicate with you. You can be hostile or work with me. It's up to you. I'll call you as soon as I know anything. You may have trouble explaining that 911 call. See if you can work something out on that. I'll do everything I can. Good-bye."

≈≈≈≈≈

As Oran Biskbey placed the phone in its cradle, it rang almost immediately. Mike Dyer was on the line.

"Karen is missing."

"Mike, what happened?"

*D.B. Cooper -aftermath-*

"We found an empty chloroform bottle outside the ladies room at the Chevron station," Mike said. "A young man is the last one who saw her."

"Cooper just called. He knows all about it."

"That son of a bitch. What does he want?"

"He said he just found about it when he called to tell her where the Donovans are."

"He's lying."

"Yeah. Why don't you come over here and stand-by? Cooper said he'd call back. I'll send a car for you."

≈≈≈≈≈

Ted removed his Nine-Millimeter-Browning from a compartment in the back of the van—he had another one in his truck—the ones he had carried in the CIA and never needed after retiring. He checked the gun, laid it on the seat beside him, got out of his van, retrieved a screwdriver from his toolbox in the back and removed the bulb on the light illuminating the license. Using his oilcan he smeared oil over the plate and threw dirt on it. Ted wiped his hands and looked at his watch not knowing what he was preparing for, no plan, nothing. He hoped she could tell him something when he called.

# SHE CALLED EVERYBODY!

After Cooper's call Karen heard doors opening and closing again and then the clanking close to her. Their hands were on her legs sliding her across the hard surface. The phone—*I must hide it.* She closed the flap. Using both hands, she tried to put the phone in the pocket of her skirt. The space was too confining with the skirt snarled around her hips. She clutched the phone.

"I'll take her," a man said. "We may need that rope, the tape and those cuffs too." He swung her around and pulled her to a sitting position. His arms circled her waist as he hefted her to his shoulder.

"Is she still out?"

"She's not moving."

In total blackness and more commotion they swung her down onto a rough hard surface.

"Mr. Barstelli! I didn't know you'd be here, "a man said.

Barstelli, she knew the name.

"Open that bag. I want to see this bitch."

*It is Barstelli. He'll kill me.* The first light came with the run of the zipper down the length of the bag as they laid it open. Six of them stared down at her—three squatting—Barstelli was standing. The glare of headlights on a car just a few feet away streamed through a pair of open swinging garage doors like those built in the twenties. Open rafters and old unfinished stud walls were turned dark with age in an empty single-car garage. Cold night air poured in. The floor was hard and rough. Her skirt had gathered around her waist. *They're going to rape me, one after the other.*

"She's okay," one of them said.

"Get her up," Barstelli said. "I've waited long enough for this."

Two of the squatting men, one on each side, grabbed her and hoisted her to her feet. Barstelli's large frame loomed in front of her.

"She's got a phone," a man said. He seized her wrist and pried the phone from her hand.

"She's probably called everybody," Barstelli said. "What's this?" He gave the lapel mike and earbob a brisk yank. The wire pulled at her blouse and dislodged the small transceiver at her waist. "Hell, she's wired. Get those clothes off."

They yanked her jacket back over her shoulders and then gave the sleeves a downward thrust over her arms to remove it. For one brief second she stood apart—free. The thrust of her foot, the point of her shoe into Barstelli's testicles, was swift and hard. The heel of her hand delivered a karate chop to another man's temple. She turned to strike again. The men piled on and pushed her to the floor—fighting and screaming. The cinder floor dug into her back.

"Tie this bitch," one of the men yelled. "String her up. Give me that rope." He came down on her to clamp her head between his knees.

Another one straddled her leg and jammed his knee into her crotch. They seized her arms to wrap the thin hemp rope three times around to tie her wrists.

A man threw the rope over a collar beam and then grabbed the dangling end. The rope tightened, her arms followed—they hauled her to her feet. She kicked. One shoe hit the stud wall. The other one tumbled across the black cinder floor packed hard with years of age.

"I need some slack," the one with the rope called. He was at the wall now.

Their hands closed around her body. Her feet dangled.

"No . . . NO," she begged.

"Okay, it's tied," the man at the wall, called.

The men eased her down until she was standing with her arms hugging close to her head. *Oh God, please help me.* The small pebbles and sharp cinders punched through her hose at the soles of her feet.

Barstelli was off to the side, stooped, hurting. *He'll grant me no mercy.*

"Lewiski's not moving," one of them said. He was sprawled on the floor. Survival training had taught her how to hit a man. The blow had struck him square on his temple.

"She hit him hard," another said. "How are you doing, Mr. Barstelli?"

Stooped over, holding himself, he grimaced in pain. "It hurts like hell." He straightened up and turned toward her. The small transceiver dangled at her waist. "Marchak, why didn't you check her out before bringing her here?"

"It's one of those wireless lapel mikes," Marchak said. "Won't go more than a few hundred feet—nobody saw us take her."

"How would you know? They may be hearing everything we say right now." His massive physique moved toward her. "Give me your knife, Marchak."

It was not large, an average size pocketknife. Straining, pulling at the tethers, she tried to avoid the open blade with no way to stop him. Rostel Barstelli began cutting and tearing, rough deliberate strokes to strip her. The cold night air pouring through the open doors enveloped her body. Sharp cinders ground into her bare feet as she struggled. Seeing the men, all focused on her, the energy centered in her throat with a fast sucking breath to scream, "YOU BASTARDS."

Barstelli's fingers hooked around her neck while his open palm covered her navel. "Don't push it. I vowed a long time ago to strip you naked if I ever had the chance and I'm not done with you yet."

The cellular phone rang. Barstelli turned, "Give me that phone." It rang again. He flipped the cap. Then, reaching over her arm, he placed the phone to her ear. Standing cheek to cheek, she listened.

"Miss Dyer, are you there?" Cooper's raspy voice.

"Answer him," Barstelli said, curling his fingers into her ribs.

" . . . Yes," she managed to say.

"Who's with you?"

She didn't answer.

Barstelli's hold on her body was unyielding. "Talk to him!"

"Who is that? You don't sound right."

"Talk to him."

"My hands are tied to a beam and he stripped me naked."

"He what?"

"They . . . the men . . . they're all around me."

"Who? . . .Who's with you?"

"Barstelli, he's right next to me standing close, listening."

"Who is this?" Barstelli said.

"What's he doing?"

"Tell him, Karen, tell him how you're squirming right now."

"Let her go. I'll give you whatever you want."

"Who are you?" Barstelli said.

"D. B. Cooper."

"What the hell do you want?"

"I want you to release Miss Dyer. I'll pay whatever you ask."

"Yeah, we'll do that, Cooper. She's not for sale."

"You saw me take three hundred thousand dollars in small unmarked bills. Miss Dyer was there."

"How will you pay us?" Barstelli said.

"We both have a problem. Neither of us wants to get caught."

"How can I call you?"

"I'll call you."

"Oh God, please help me."

"What are you doing to her?"

"I'm giving her a thrill, Cooper. Tell him, Karen, tell him what I'm doing to you."

"You bastard," she said throwing her head back to scream, "no NO." Pushing away, her toes dug into the cinders.

"Get the money, Cooper. Call me."

"It's ready. Untie her and let her have her clothes."

"Yeah. There are some things I need to know before you call."

"Don't hurt her. I'll give you whatever you want."

A snap of the flap ended the call. Barstelli handed the phone to one of the men. "What's between you and this Cooper guy?"

"Nothing." Her head dropped forward. The tension on her arms increased as her body sagged.

Barstelli grabbed her hair, pulled her head back and slapped her face. "He knew you were going to answer when he called."

"What's he want?" the one he had called Marchak said.

"Cooper's willing to pay three hundred grand for her."

"Do you think he'll pay that kind of money?"

"He has the hots for her. He'll call back."

"She's seen all of us," Marchak said. "The deal was to ship her out of the country."

"After we deal with Cooper we'll use her to take care of the other matter. Lewiski's moving, is he all right?"

"He's starting to come out of it," one of the men said and then added. "How are you doing?"

"She got me good in the nuts," Barstelli said as he looked straight into her eyes with his face just inches away, his hand still entwined in her hair. "I had to run for my life because of you."

"Four of our men are in jail because of her," one of the men said.

"That's the other matter I was talking about," Barstelli said as he stared at her. "You know I can hurt you bad?"

"No . . . please."

"What's between you and Cooper?"

"He . . . he called me in New York and told me he had kidnapped Senator Donovan and his wife. It . . .it was a breaking story and I came to Portland to cover it. If you watched the coverage, you saw it all."

"And you never knew Cooper before?"

"That's right." She was hurting and angry now.

"And he's ready to put out big bucks for you?"

"I . . . I don't know anything about that!"

Barstelli stepped away, her head fell forward as her body slumped, hanging on the rope. "Cut her down and put her in the body bag. We're moving out."

"No, please . . . not in the bag," she said, reaching, trying to relieve the strain.

Barstelli turned back. "Honey, we're going to take good care of you. Be thankful you're still alive." He turned away in a stooped posture—hurting. "Leave her hands tied and hobble those ankles. Put her in that bag. Take her to the Cad."

"You going to Carol's house?" one of the men said.

"Yeah, you and Joe follow Lewiski and me in the pickup."

"You said five-thousand on delivery," Marchak said.

"Pay him, Lewiski."

# THE BACK SEAT

The total blackness of the body bag entombed her as she sat naked in the back seat of a car with the seat belt pulled snug over her shoulder and lap with her wrists tied and a short hobble around her ankles. She listened. The man she hit—the one they called Lewiski was driving. Barstelli was in the right seat.

"What are you going to say when he calls," Lewiski said.

"I'm going to take his money, there's no risk. He can't go to the police. Cooper's three hundred thousand is a freebee."

"I do believe Marchak picked her up clean," Lewiski said. "We just don't know why this Cooper guy is willing to pay so much money for her. She wasn't wired, you know."

"Yeah, Marchak's okay but I thought he blew it when I saw that wire in her jacket. I'm still hurting where she kicked me."

"It was so quick. She laid me out cold. Do you think she knows more than she's telling?"

"Yeah,.we'll talk to her again after we get to the house."

The phone rang. Barstelli answered.

"Yeah."

She listened.

"What kind of a deal?"

*It must be Cooper.*

"How are you going to do that?"

Karen shifted on the seat. The rough material scuffed her flesh. Her wrists and ankles throbbed. The bag fit so close.

"Sure, I'll do that Cooper. I'll rush right down there. How soon can you be in Kelso?"

*What was he saying?*

"Call me, I'll tell you where to go from there."

Another pause. *He must have hung-up.*

"He wants us to bring her to Ariel, says he may have as much as a half-million. We'll send Marty and Joe to Kelso to collect the money. Marty knows that area. It'll be an easy pickup."

"We passed through Kelso ten minutes ago."

"Yeah, I know. Pull over; we need to talk with Marty and Joe."

The car slowed. *Joe and Marty must be pulling up behind.*

His voice was louder. *He must be looking back through the rear window.* The car eased to a stop. A door opened.

"What's up?" a man said. He was outside.

"Marty, I want you and Joe to go back to Kelso and take care of Cooper," Barstelli said. He too was outside of the car now. "He's got three hundred grand, maybe a half million in cash. Pick it up and bring it to Carol's house."

"What's the plan?"

"There isn't one. Cooper called a few minutes ago. He wants to trade the money for the Dyer woman. He's got the hots for her and he can't go to the police. He was an hour away from Kelso so you'll be there before him. He'll call you when he's there. You know the area so set up something. Get the money and dispose of him. You won't have any trouble."

"But you're going to keep her with you?"

"Yeah."

"Are you sure he hasn't called someone. The whole country may be looking for her."

"He can't expose himself. Check it out before you make your move. If it looks okay, take him."

"He may want to see her."

"Oh, I'm sure he will. When you get that close, you can make your move. You know the terrain. If it doesn't feel right, back away from it. He's going to call you on this phone. Here— take it—get going. Come to Carol's as soon as you've taken care of Cooper."

~~~~~

Mike Dyer waited with Chief Biskbey and six officers in plain clothes in the chief's office at the Portland police station. It had been thirty minutes since Cooper had called. Two unmarked cars were ready.

*Dear God, please be with Karen wherever she is.*

~~~~~

Ted looked at his watch—ten more minutes before he could call. Those last words, *we have some things to find out*—I'm standing naked with my hands tied to a beam, lingered in his mind. *God, what if it was Molly? I'll kill the bastards.*

Ted had lied to her kidnappers when he told them he was an hour out of Kelso. He could make it in half of that. After talking to her and her abductors, he called Biskbey. He wasn't happy. Mike Dyer was also on the line. "I'm trying to make a deal with her abductors," he told Biskbey. "Did you cover your bases on that 911 call?"

"We told them it was a crank call, some smart-ass calling."

"And the media accepted that?"

"Yeah, for now anyway."

After talking to Biskbey, Ted headed south on Interstate 5. He'd be in Kelso in fifteen minutes. It had only been twenty minutes since he talked to her kidnappers. He had waited long enough. He punched the number. The phone from locker 102 rang twice.

"Hello."

It wasn't the same man he had talked to before. "This is D. B. Cooper. Who is this?"

"Don't be funny, where are you?"

"I'm forty minutes out of Kelso. You're not the same man I talked to before, the one who told me to go to Kelso."

"He's here."

"Let me talk to him and Miss Dyer."

"Never mind about Dyer, I'll do the talking from now on."

"I see. What's the plan?" Ted said. She's not with him, he was sure of that.

"Do you have all the money?"

"Yes. Is Miss Dyer all right?"

"She's okay. I was told that you may have a half million."

"Yeah, a half million," Ted said. "Did you give her some clothes?"

"You just worry about delivering that money and then she's all yours," the man said. "Give me a number; I'll call you in ten minutes."

"I'll call you. You can't call out on that phone."

"I've got another phone."

"I'll call you in ten minutes," Ted said as he closed the cap.

≈≈≈≈

Marty and Joe were approaching Longview just west of Kelso traveling east on State Road 4. They could see the lights of the city.

"This guy's not as dumb as Barstelli made out." Marty said

"Do you think it's a trap?"

"No, I don't think so. He wants her back. Like Barstelli said, he can't go to the police . . . There's a little league baseball field ahead on the west edge of Longview near the Three Rivers Shopping Center Mall. It's almost closing time and there won't be many people around at this hour. I'm going to pull off and look at that ball field."

As Marty turned left off State Road 4 and then right onto a frontage road, the lights of the Three Rivers Shopping Center were visible in the distance. "The ball-field is on the left side before we get to the shopping center," Marty said peering through the windshield. He spotted the tall screen behind home plate fifty feet off of the narrow blacktop frontage road. He turned left—then another hard left, a full U-turn, back toward third base. He pulled into a parking place adjacent to third base. A three-foot chain link fence, parallel to the third base line, separated the parking spaces from the ball field.

The headlights on his truck illuminated the field and the pitcher's mound. Another fence and more parking spaces paralleled the first base line to the right—just barely perceptible at the far reaches of the truck's headlights. Marty turned his headlights out and the sky became totally black with every star showing bright. "What do you think?"

"It's dark and secluded."

"That frontage road terminates at the entrance to the shopping mall. We can see the lights of anyone approaching from either direction."

"Barstelli said to back off if it doesn't look right," Marty said, looking at his watch. "Cooper should be calling soon."

～～～～

Ted Bolan pulled off the freeway at the Kelso exit into a mini-mart parking lot. It wouldn't hurt to get some gas, he thought. He paid cash for the gas. He punched in the number on his cell phone. It rang once.

"Is this Cooper?" the man said.

"Yes."

"Where are you?"

"Twenty-five minutes from Kelso," Ted said.

"When you get to Kelso, drive west on State Road 4 through Longview. When you get to 46$^{th}$ Avenue, call me." The line went dead.

Ted reached for his Browning on the seat beside him to be sure it was ready and then laid a flashlight and the New York cellular phone beside it. He was still wearing the bib overalls. He removed them and put on his black clothes. He retrieved his big parka and slipped his felt hood into one of the inside pockets. Then he proceeded west on State Road 4 toward Longview.

# Carol's House

Sitting naked in a bag with her hands and feet tied, Karen Dyer had lost all concept of time, except that the ride seemed endless. After talking with Marty and Joe and sending them on their quest, Barstelli and Lewiski were on the road again. The pain in her arms and shoulders had subsided to a dull ache. The car slowed, made some turns and then stopped. The doors opened. They released the seat belt and pulled her out. Her body slung like a hammock as they carried her. She heard another door.

"What's that?" . . . a woman's voice.

"It's Karen Dyer," Barstelli said.

"The woman on TV?" The woman's voice again.

Karen felt the hard floor and then heard the rip of the zipper. The light streamed in. Lewiski squatted beside her. Barstelli and a woman were standing, staring down at her, a blowzy blond, mid thirties, pretty enough in a showgirl kind of way.

"She's naked."

"Yeah, she's naked," Barstelli said.

They seized Karen's arms and lifted her to her feet.

"There's a bathroom down the hall," Barstelli said pointing.

"You've tied my hands."

"You can manage." Barstelli said smacking her on the buttocks. "GO. Lewiski will go with you."

"You bastard," she said.

"Yeah, you said that before."

She almost fell when he shoved her back into Lewiski's arms. The hobble was no more than ten, maybe twelve inches.

"Get her something to eat when she comes out." Barstelli said to the woman.

"I'm not hungry," Karen said.

"You do as you're told," Barstelli said. Lewiski was right behind her.

"Your man is so tough next to a tied-up woman."

"Go to the bathroom," Barstelli said pushing her to the side toward the bathroom. "Take care of her, Lewiski."

"Do you want me to get her some clothes?" the woman said.

"No. Put her in the small bedroom and tie her hands to the head of the bed."

# THE NEGOTIATING

Ted Bolan arrived at 46$^{th}$ Avenue and punched in the number. The same man answered.
"Cooper?"
"Yes."
"Where are you?"
"On State Road 4 at 46$^{th}$ Avenue."
"Then you can see the lights of the shopping Center?"
"Off to the right?"
"Yeah, that's the Three Rivers Shopping Center."
"I see it."
Drive west on State Road 4, to the corner. Turn right as though you were going into the center then turn left onto the frontage road. Watch for a baseball field, you'll see the tall screen behind home plate. Turn right and go straight down the first-base line and park with your headlights on. Put the money where I can see it. After you do that, get in your car and wait in the shopping center."
"When do I see Miss Dyer?"
"As soon I verify the money I'll send her to the center on foot."
"I need to see her before I put the money out."
"If you want to see her alive, you'll put that money out where I can see it. We'll have a real good time with her if you don't. It's the only deal you're going to get."

"I'll move as fast as I can," Ted said closing the cover on his cell phone. They didn't have her, he was sure of that. *It didn't seem like an ordinary rape and run, there is more to it than he knew.* He'd have to hurry. He drove to the shopping center and parked among other cars.

He grabbed the keys. The felt hood was in the pocket of his parka. He cocked his Browning Nine Millimeter to place a round in the chamber before putting it into a pocket. He grabbed his flashlight and locked the van. No need to take the briefcase with the money, *she's not with them.*

He walked briskly to the edge of the parking lot and then toward the frontage road. He stayed in the shadows. The man said it wasn't far. The dark night made him virtually invisible. Not knowing what he might need, he was glad he hadn't washed the makeup off his face and hands. He could barely make out the big screen behind home plate against a dark moonless sky.

He crept up behind the screen and saw a faint outline of a pickup truck near third base. He circled back to the road and into the brush—behind the truck. Two men were in the cab. Was it possible she might be in the back? He didn't think so. He flipped the cell phone open and shielded the lighted dial to punch in the number. It rang twice. Ted saw the man put the phone to his ear.

"Yeah."

"This is Cooper."

"Where are you?"

"Down by first base where you told me to be."

"I didn't see you."

"It's dark."

"I told you to drive in with your headlights on."

"I turned my lights off and parked out on the road. I want to see Miss Dyer first."

"I have to see the money."

"I have it. The briefcase is in my hand."

"Cooper, I'm gonna kill her."

"No please, I'm putting the money on the ground now just like you told me."

"I have to see it."

"I'll shine a flashlight on it." He closed the cap on the cell phone.

The right door opened and the dome light gave Bolan his first good look at the two men.

"Come on. He says he's over by first base," he heard the man say. The other door opened and both men were out with their guns drawn. They moved along the fence line toward the big screen behind home plate.

Ted reached for his Browning without taking it from the pocket. The two men crept cautiously.

Rising from the brush, Ted moved toward their truck. Climbing over the side, he huddled in the right front corner of the truck bed and listened. Then suddenly, they weren't creeping cautiously any longer, they were charging back toward the truck.

"It's a trap," one of them said. They scrambled into the cab.

Ted laid flat, doors slammed, wheels spun. The truck backed out and then lunged forward making that full U turn onto on the frontage road and then a left and right. to State Road 4.

The wind whistled loudly as Ted pulled his parka around his neck.

≈≈≈≈≈

"I don't think we're being followed," Joe said staring back through the rear window.

"What do you think he was doing back there?" Marty eased back to fifty as the road narrowed to a two-lane country road.

"Sure looked like a setup."

"Right."

≈≈≈≈≈

Barstelli was restless. One long wall of the room was glass, floor to ceiling—a large room, thirty feet long and half as wide. A massive fireplace in a stone wall at one end had smoldering embers that radiated heat into the room. Barstelli rose from his seat and tossed two logs on the fire. The television played softly. The Columbia River was seventy feet away. A boat dock, illuminated by single yard light, was barely visible.

He liked coming to the United States but he knew the danger. He always had to travel in secrecy, never sure whom he could trust. After the trial starts, it's going to get worse. It worried him now that so many people knew he was here. If he was caught, they had him dead to rights and he knew it. He picked up the phone and called his pilot. "Be ready to roll at six in the morning."

Carol Fleming didn't like South America. He hadn't seen her in four months. She'd cut and run if he stopped providing money. *Who was she seeing on the side?* She had been home alone when Barstelli and Lewiski arrived earlier this afternoon and somewhat annoyed that he hadn't called. "How does she always know when I'm coming," Lewiski said later.

"I'll kill'em both if I ever find her with another man," Barstelli said. "It may be time to terminate her. She knows too much about my business."

"If something happened to her, they'd go into her books and they might find a lot of things," Lewiski said.

Damn, Barstelli thought, what an impossible situation.

# THE RIDE

Lying in the back of the truck, Ted couldn't chance looking ahead so he saw everything after they passed. He figured they had traveled about thirty minutes and he was reasonably certain they had not passed through Cathlamet.

The truck slowed, making a left turn. There were lights—a town. The truck speeded up and then slowed again before making a right turn and easing to a stop. He lay still across the front of the truck bed. The two men got out and walked away. He stayed low listening to the crickets and trees rustling gently—the sounds of the night.

Cautiously he peered over the rim of the bed. The truck was in the driveway of a large house fifty feet away with a few lighted windows. A light-colored sedan was parked nearby, a Cadillac. The house sat back a hundred feet or more from the road.

He moved to the left side of the truck, the side away from the house, climbed out and crept behind some shrubbery. The house was long and rambling, all on one floor. He had to find out where he was. With a watchful eye he stood and walked toward the road. The rural mailbox had large numbers, *10267.* On top of the box big cast letters spelled *FLEMING.*

Looking down the road a thousand feet away he could see the lights of a town, the same lights he saw when the truck passed through. Walking toward the lights the matching fences on both sides of the road implied that it was all one piece of property with no other houses—more like a private drive than a street. At the corner he saw a convenience store with gas pumps out front. He looked for a street sign. There was none.

He pushed the hood of the parka back behind his head and pulled his baseball cap down on his forehead before entering the store. He spotted a small hardware section, a candy rack in front of the register and fresh brewed coffee. The clock on the wall indicated ten thirty-five.

He went to the hardware section first, he needed an ice pick. A pocketknife—he might need one.

He put some powdered cream in the bottom of a large cup and thought of Molly as he poured the coffee. *She'd never learn to put the cream in first so it would mix automatically when pouring.* He placed the items on the counter. He liked Snicker candy bars and took one. As the young lady rang the sale, he read the address on the store license:

Cathlamet, WA

After receiving change, he asked, "What's the name of this street out there?" He pointed.

"Harwood Street," the young lady said.

"The matching fences make it like a private drive."

"It used to be a street but it is a private drive now."

"Thank you," he said, turning and leaving the store. He stood in the shadows. The coffee tasted good and he ate the candy bar. He thought of Molly and wished there was someway to relieve her mind. There was no way he would use the New York cellular phone to call her. Molly would have to wait.

He sipped the last of his coffee and started walking toward the Fleming house, then he stopped and returned to the public phone booth outside the store.

*Why can't they design something better to hold a phone book?* They're so awkward, particularly when holding a flashlight. He was into the *F's—Fleming.* There weren't many. There it was: *Carol Fleming at 10267 Harwood Street.* He underlined number before tearing part of the page from the phone book.

Quietly he made his way back and circled to the back of the house. The property fronted on the Columbia River. A yard light shined on a distant boat dock. Houses on the far bank a half mile away with lighted windows were visible.

The back wall of a room was all glass, floor to ceiling, with a sliding glass door in the middle. Four men and a woman were in the room. The television was on—they weren't watching it. Ted took the cell phone from his pocket and entered the number for the phone from locker 102. They stirred. One of the men took a phone from his coat pocket and handed it to another man. He answered, "Who is this?"

It was the same man he had talked to the first time when he talked to Karen Dyer—the same man who stripped her and said he had things to find out. Her words, *I'm standing naked tied to a beam,* reverberated through his mind. "I'm D. B. Cooper."

"Where the hell are you?"

I'm at the Three Rivers Shopping Center in Longview," Ted said.

"You didn't follow instructions."

"What are you bastards trying to pull? I dropped the money and you guys took off. Where's Karen Dyer?"

"My men said you tried to set a trap. We're not dealing with you anymore. Karen Dyer's our baby now."

"I'm not hearing you too well, I'll call you back on Carol's phone," Ted said, closing the flap, turning and moving away in the darkness.

≈≈≈≈≈

Barstelli eased the phone away from his ear and closed the flap to lay the cell phone aside.

"What'd he say, where is he?" Lewiski said.

"At the three Rivers Shopping Center . . . said he'd call back on Carol's phone." Turning to Carol, "Where'd you meet this guy?"

"I don't know what you're talking about."

"Don't lie to me."

"I'm not lying . . . I don't know anything about it."

"He said he'd call back on your phone."

"I don't know what you're talking about," she repeated.

"How'd he know your name?"

"I don't know," she said, sinking to the couch burying her face in her hands.

# The Shoot Out

Moving cautiously, Ted returned to the front of the house where the truck and the sedan were parked. He placed the point of the ice pick against the sidewall of a tire and hit the handle with the palm of his hand to make it enter. When he pulled it out he listened for escaping air. He repeated the process on all four tires on both vehicles before returning to the rear of the house. The four men were still there—standing—talking. The man he had just talked to had a drink in his hand. The woman was sitting on the couch, slumped over.

Ted took the felt hood from his pocket and pulled it snugly over his head and replaced his baseball cap. He flipped the safety off on his nine-millimeter. Then, just to be sure, he checked the listing on the torn page from the phone book before entering Carol Fleming's phone number.

≈≈≈≈

Barstelli looked down at Carol Fleming while speaking to Lewiski. "You say she's been gone two weeks at a time."

"That has nothing to do with this," she said, not giving Lewiski time to answer—burying her face in her hands—crying.

"Then you do know him."

"No," she screamed looking up at him and then burying her face in her hands again. "I don't know anything about all this."

The phone rang—the one on the end table. Barstelli grabbed it. "Hello!"

"This is me."

"Where in the hell did you get this number?"

"Carol gave it to me."

Barstelli slammed the phone down. "The son of a bitch knows where we are," he said reaching down and seizing Carol by the front of her blouse.

"Aaaaah," she screamed loud and long.

"Who is this guy?" he said pulling her to her feet and arching over her.

"No no, I don't know what you're talking about!"

"What's going on?" Lewiski said.

"She told him where we are. We got to get out of here. Get the Dyer woman."

Marty and Joe turned and ran toward the bedroom.

"I didn't tell him anything!" she screamed.

"You lying bitch, you were itching to get me." He drew his gun and held it just inches from her face.

"No, no please. I didn't do it!"

He fired one time. The back of her head exploded. "Bring the Dyer woman! We're moving out."

≈≈≈≈≈

"My God, he shot her," Ted muttered. Then he saw Karen Dyer stark naked between two men, twisting, straining and bucking in their grasp. Ted fired a shot into the air.

≈≈≈≈≈

"What was that?" Barstelli yelled—turning—looking.

"It's outside," Lewiski said, drawing his gun.

Marty and Joe held Karen Dyer with their guns ready.

"He's out there," Barstelli said. "Let me have her." He grabbed and spun her around in front of him and clamped his arm over her throat—pushing her ahead toward the door and pressing the gun into her ear.

She screamed loud and long.

"Open the door. Let's get this guy!"

Marty slid the door. Barstelli charged out pushing her ahead. She reared back—screaming.

"Come on Cooper, you wanta play games!"

≈≈≈≈≈

*The man's crazy—he killed that woman.* Seeing her twisting nude body made Ted draw down. The bucking and rearing deflected the man's gun hand away from her head. *She was only fifteen feet away. He couldn't miss.* Ted squeezed the trigger. The man's head veered violently to one side when the hollow point slug exploded. He fell taking Karen Dyer down on him, screaming as she fell.

≈≈≈≈≈

"He shot Barstelli," Marty yelled.

"Let's get out of here," Lewiski said turning away from the sliding door.

"Who has the keys to the Caddy?" Marty yelled.

"I gave them to Carol, We'll have to take the truck," Lewiski said.

Lewiski, Joe and Marty charged to the foyer and through the door to the front yard.

Marty jumped into the driver's seat as Joe and Lewiski entered the right side. The engine started. The lights were on.

He shoved it in reverse and gunned it hard. The trucked lurched and one wheel went off the driveway.

"I can't steer it. Something's wrong," Marty said.

"You're going off the driveway into shrubbery," Lewiski said.

Marty threw it in drive and the truck lunged forward. Lewiski and Joe jumped out. "The left front tire is flat," Lewiski said.

"We got two flat ones over here!" Joe said. "We'll have to take Carol's other car."

"In the garage?"

"Yeah, you'll have to get this truck out of the way," Lewiski said racing toward the house.

≈≈≈≈≈

Falling on Barstelli, Karen scrambled to get away on hobbled feet.

"Over here," she heard him say. She saw the hooded figure crouching in the shadows. She managed to rise to her knees.

"Get his gun."

"I can't, my feet and hands are tied." The hooded figure moved toward her. She tried to get away falling forward. He grabbed her from behind and turned her body to look into her face.

"It's okay, it's over. You're safe now."

"I'm so cold."

Pushing her away and reaching in his pocket, he said, "Put your hands out."

She felt the grasp of his hand as he cut the cords to release her wrists and ankles.

"Your wrists have some bad bruises, He slipped his parka back over his shoulders.

"My hands are numb."

"This parka is the best I can do." He held it as she slipped into it.

"Thank you." She saw his black clothing, the same clothes he had worn at the bank.

"It's a magnificent gesture on my part. The view was better before."

*It was not a lewd remark; he meant it, a compliment. I'm safe with him.*

He handed her a handkerchief to wipe her face. "Are you up to using that gun?" He gestured toward the gun near Barstelli's hand as she buttoned the parka.

"I know exactly how to use it." She reached for it. The safety was already off. Her adrenalin was flowing and she wasn't cold anymore.

"Let's go."

"Where?" She did feel the cold air around her legs and feet as she stepped out onto the damp grass.

"Around in front, we have to get those guys before they circle around to get us. How many are there?"

"Three now." She heard the engine racing. "They're leaving."

"No, they're still here."

"The engines?"

"They won't go far."

*How does he know?* Following close, crouching with Barstelli's gun in her hand, she watched Cooper peek around the front corner of the house. She crept up behind him.

The truck beside the Caddy lunged and wallowed—the headlights swept in their direction. Cooper fired two shots. The lights were out.

"Move and you're dead."

The garage door began to rise and the overhead light came on. One man was in the truck. Another man, the one they called Joe, was standing near the right front wheel. A third man, Lewiski, stood just inside the garage. He turned.

"Did you see . . . ?"

"I saw him," Cooper said as he fired a shot into the casing of the door. "You stand fast."

Lewiski froze.

"I'm going to crawl over there." Cooper gestured to his left away from the house. Lying flat he crawled across the grass. She saw Joe looking toward Cooper, raising his gun to take aim. With both hands, she leveled Barstelli's gun and fired. The impact of the bullet sent him reeling into the fender.

Lewiski turned to run. She fired. The bullet smashed into the garage wall—just inches from Lewiski. He stopped.

"You move again and you're dead," Cooper Yelled. On your belly . . . now. . . hands above your head—put that gun on the pavement."

Lewiski dropped to the pavement reaching high, shoving his gun aside.

"All right, you in the truck, get moving to that garage door."

The man she shot, Joe, lay sprawled on his back. Marty got out of the truck and turned to run. Cooper fired. Marty cried out and fell, holding his knee.

"Get over to that garage door," Cooper said.

"My knee's busted."

"Crawl, get over there, NOW." Cooper fired again, just inches from his head.

Marty crawled, pulling himself ahead on his hands and one knee toward Lewiski.

"We have a bead on both of you. If you two guys want to live stay on you bellies with hands high above your heads. Then, looking down at Joe, "This one's dead. You hit him square in the chest."

"That's exactly where I aimed." For just one split second the light reflected past his glasses under the fitted hood and she saw his eyes. They were a team.

"You have a phone in the pocket of that coat—give it to me."

She handed the phone to him. He punched in a number with his thumb.

"Chief, we are in Cathlamet, Washington. There's a convenience store. It's the only store open. Turn left and look for an open garage door on your right. The mail box has 10267 on it. . . . .She's okay. I have her here beside me." He closed the flap and slipped the phone into his pants pocket. "Biskbey is on his way. Are you sure there's nobody else in that house?"

"I don't think so."

"Why don't you go in the house and find some clothes. Take the gun with you. If somebody shows up, I'll have to leave so get back as soon as you can.

She walked into the garage past Lewiski and Marty. A pool of blood had formed under his knee.

≈≈≈≈≈

He watched her go; the parka barely covered her hips. A beautiful lady standing naked tied to a beam—*those bastards.* He turned toward the men on their bellies. *It would not take much to make me shoot them here and now.*

He clamped his arms against his ribs to ward off the chill as he looked around. Apparently no one had heard the shots. The convenience store was the closest building and it was more than a thousand feet away. He didn't want company. Biskbey was a good hour away but he could call someone. If anybody showed up, he'd have to disappear into the darkness.

"I need help," the man said. "I'm bleeding and it hurts."

Ted saw the puddle of blood on the pavement. "You just lay quiet and think about what you did."

# BLUE SLACKS

As Karen stepped into the house from the garage she saw the woman they had called Carol laying on the floor with her head on a blood-soaked carpet. She glanced at the open sliding door where Barstelli had fallen. The embers in the fireplace at the far end of the room crackled and glowed red. She looked into the other bedrooms just to be sure.

In the master bedroom she laid Barstelli's gun on the bed and slipped the large parka back over her shoulders. The bruises on her wrists had turned to a nasty dark purple showing the imprint of every turn of the thin hemp rope. Her ankles had marks but not nearly as bad. Then, going into the bathroom, she turned the shower on and waited for hot water. She stepped in and allowed the spray to pour down over her face.

≈≈≈≈≈

Ted saw her coming. She was wearing light blue slacks with a matching coat over a beige blouse. His parka was slung over her arm. She laid Barstelli's gun on the hood of the truck and handed him his coat.

One of the men stirred. "Don't even think about it," Ted said. Then, turning to Karen Dyer, "why did they kidnap you? What were they after?"

"Barstelli and the one called Lewiski, talked about that while I was in the back of the car coming here. They were afraid of all the stuff that'll come out at the upcoming trial if the men started plea-bargaining. Barstelli wanted me as a hostage—that and the fact he hated me."

"Barstelli?"

"He's the one who was holding me when you shot him."

"Which one's Lewiski?"

"The one without the busted knee—the one that stirred a moment ago."

"You knew them?"

"Not Lewiski, I interviewed Barstelli eight months ago."

"Come on, grab your gun." Ted walked to the man she had identified as Lewiski and knelt on one knee. "Roll over."

With Karen also kneeling, Ted nudged the man and inserted the barrel into Lewiski's mouth.

"Shove your gun into his testicles, Miss Dyer. Make him feel it."

"What are you doing?"

"Lewiski wants to tell us a few things." Ted seized Lewiski's hair to shove his head against the pavement. "Have you ever seen a man with his testicles blown off? Cock your gun, Miss Dyer, make him feel it." Lewiski made a gurgling sound and Ted eased off a bit with his black hood just inches above Lewiski's face. "Now, there are a couple of things I want to know." Lewiski's eyes were open wide and Ted could see the fear.

"Now, tell me, why did you abduct Miss Dyer?" Ted slowly withdrew his gun and then pushed the muzzle up against his nose.

"I . . . I was told to do it."

"I want names. Make it hurt Miss Dyer."

"Stark called me and I called Barstelli. He said to get Marchak to pick her up. He told me to offer thirty-five grand if he could pick her up alive."

"Who's Marchak?"

"He and Angelli run the Portland operation."

"And if he couldn't pick her up alive?"

"Twenty if he had to kill her."

"Who's Stark?"

"I just know him by Stark."

Cooper turned to Karen.

"Roger Stark is Senator Donovan's attorney," Karen said.

Then, staring down at Lewiski, Ted said, "Donovan and Roger Stark are in business with you guys?"

"Barstelli had them on a retainer."

"What about Bowers?" Karen said. "Ask him about Bowers."

"The Director of the FBI?" Ted said, turning, looking at Karen Dyer but still holding Lewiski's head with the gun against his nostrils.

"I've suspected him for sometime but we could never get a closure," Karen Dyer said. "The way Barstelli responded in that interview tended to implicate him."

"What about that, Lewiski?" Ted said, looking down on him.

"Carol sent money to Stark in Washington every quarter to distribute."

"Carol?" Bolan said.

"She and Barstelli lived together until he went to South America after the warrants were issued. She took care of the details and kept the books."

"That the woman he shot?" Ted said as he pushed the gun just a bit harder.

"Yeah."

"Where are those books?" Karen Dyer said.

"Tell her," Ted said.

"She has an accounting business in Seattle, Fleming and Associates."

"Anything else?" Ted said, turning to Karen.

"Tell me more about that accounting business and her relation to Barstelli."

Lewiski hesitated. Ted shoved his gun forcing Lewiski's head back on the pavement.

"It's a business her father started and she took it over after he died before she met Barstelli, before he moved into her house."

"How long ago was that?" Karen said.

"Long time, seven, eight, nine years maybe."

"Anything else, Mrs. Dyer."

"No."

"Consider yourself lucky, Lewiski," Ted said. "Roll over on your belly and keep those hands high."

Moving back to the truck, Karen said, "I suspected them for a long time but this makes it conclusive."

"Donovan killed his first wife," Ted said.

"A lot of people believe that."

"Andrew Phillips is serving a life sentence for two murders. He would have received the death sentence if the powers to be hadn't intervened. I think it came straight from Senator Donovan. Phillips was a police officer in Washington D. C. On the side he was a hired killer. He knew how to fix things."

"How do you know all these things?"

Ignoring her question, Ted added, "Ask Phillips why Dr. Tina Mathews mysteriously changed her testimony after releasing an autopsy report that would have convicted the Senator. Ask him what happened to her two days after the inquest."

"Tina Mathews moved away. It's part of the record," Karen said.

"She was twenty-nine years old with a new husband and a career as a very successful pathologist. Almost ten years have gone by without a trace of her. Check the file and then ask Andrew Phillips the right questions. After eight years in prison, with no hope of parole, I think he might tell you a few things."

"You seem to know a lot about the case."

"Just follow-up, you'll see for yourself. Do you know your husband's cell phone number?"

"Yes,"

"Here, call him." Ted handed her the phone.

She entered the number. He must have answered on the first ring, Ted thought.

"Yes, I'm all right . . . He's right here beside me" . . . "In thirty minutes, you'll be here in thirty minutes? . . He didn't tell me that."

She closed the flap and handed the phone back.

"You didn't tell me he was with Biskbey."

"No, I guess I didn't."

"You haven't really told me anything about yourself."

"You've already seen and heard far more than I wanted you to. Why does CBS give scum bums like Senator Donovan the favorable publicity they seek?" Ted's tone of voice had anger and there was no lisp or rasp. He liked Karen Dyer and had nothing to fear from her. "You people manufacture news instead of reporting it. Free press, yes but do it without all the adjectives."

"It sells and we are in a very competitive business."

"That's right, our whole political spectrum is that way. Donovan is not a good Senator and it angered me when I read about his party on the same day as the attack on the World Trade Center. The victims will receive Donovan's twenty-five million dollars." He paused. "And one other thing, why aren't people who happen to be victims through no fault of their own just as entitled to receive assistance as someone who just happened to be in the World Trade Center on that day?" Again, he paused. "Now you know why I did it."

She didn't respond.

"I think you can handle this now," he said. "Don't take your eyes off of them."

"Where are you going?"

"I'm leaving. Somebody'll be pulling in here any minute now. I'll call and tell you where the Donovans are as soon as I'm clear."

"I had forgotten about them."

"Yeah, the Senator's a scumbag. Remember that the next time you're interviewing and couching your questions a certain way for millions of people to see and hear." He turned and walked into the darkness.

"I'd still like to see what you look like."

He stopped, turned back. "You saw me in New York City. It was at a banquet at that Rotary meeting many years ago when you were a cub reporter. I met your husband too."

"You know Mike?"

"No but we met one time."

Walking into the blackness, he turned again and looked back. He could see her silhouette framed in the open garage door. "If somebody calls and offers you a Barbi Doll, accept the call."

Staying low he hurried. One car, a late model, was parked in front of the convenience store. The clerk and a man were in the store. Ted tried the right door of the car. It was unlocked. He took a hundred-dollar bill out of his wallet. That's when he heard the siren and saw the flashing red lights approaching. He moved quickly around the corner of the store into the shadows. The man and the clerk ran out and watched two Clark County Sheriff cars speed around the corner. The two men moved to within a few feet of the spot where Ted crouched to watch the two cars turn into the Fleming drive way.

Ted lay tight against the wall. Finally, the clerk returned to the store. The man went to his car. As he slid into the left side, Ted opened the right door with his gun in hand. "Here's a hundred dollar bill. It's yours. I want you to drive east on State Road 4."

"Okay, don't shoot me."

"I don't plan to hurt you, or take anything from you. Just take me to Longview."

≈≈≈≈

Karen saw the two police cars coming and watched them skid to a stop behind the disabled truck and Cad. The light from the open garage illuminated their faces as Sheriff Grant Taylor and the other officers stepped out and moved quickly toward her.

"It's been almost eighteen years since those high school days, Grant," she said as he approached.

"Oh, I see you most every day on TV."

"You haven't changed that much." She reached out to shake his hand.

"Chief Bisbey called and told me where to find you."

"They are coming, aren't they?" Karen said.

"He and your husband will be here soon."

≈≈≈≈

Mike was first out of the car. They held each other close and then stepping apart holding hands he saw her wrists below the sleeves of the jacket. "He hurt you didn't he?"

"No Mike, it was Barstelli and his men. They hurt me but I'm all right. That's where they tied me but I'm okay."

"I think we should get you checked over."

"Mike, I'm all right. Nothing's broken."

"Where is he?" Biskbey asked.

"He's gone."

"When?"

"About thirty minutes ago," she said. "Just before Sheriff Taylor arrived."

"On foot?"

"Yes."

"Let's go after him."

She smiled, without releasing Mike's hands, enjoying the whole thing. "Which way you going to look, Chief? You'd need a hundred men to search the area."

He peered into the blackness. "Yeah, I see what you mean but he is on foot."

"He still has the Donovans." She saw the grin on Biskbey's face as she remembered their conversation. *I bet he gets away.*

"He didn't tell you where they are?" Mike said.

"He's going to call in an hour."

"That's where we were five hours ago," Mike said. "This time I'm not letting you out of my sight."

# HE'S GONE

The late model car, which Ted had commandeered, approached Longview. "Turn here and follow the frontage road," he said, pointing. The shopping center parking lot, where he had left his van, was virtually empty. "Stop here. Turn around in that drive." Ted gestured toward the entrance of the deserted little league field.

"It's . . . it's awfully dark," the man said with a tremble in his voice as he maneuvered the car.

"Do you have a cell phone?"

"No."

Ted held his gun where the man could see it. "Go back the way we came. Don't stop, I'll be watching you." He opened the door and got out, "Go."

The car sped away. Ted walked to his van and then drove east on State Road 4 to Interstate 5. The digital clock on the dash of his van indicated 2:32, just under an hour since he left Karen Dyer. She didn't have the phone from locker 102. He looked at his pad and entered Mike Dyer's cellular phone number.

"This is Mike."

"Mr. Dyer, go east on State Road 503 to the Ariel turnoff. Continue east another 5.2 miles to an obscure gravel drive. There is an old log cabin to the right a hundred feet off the road. That's where the Senator and his wife are. You may have a little trouble finding it. Check your odometer as you pass the Ariel turn-off."

"A hundred feet off the road?"

"That's right, 5.2 miles past the Ariel turn-off on the south side. How's your wife doing?"

"She's all right."

"I'm sorry for what happened. I wish you, your wife and your family the very best. This is the last time you will hear from D. B. Cooper."

~~~~~

"Go 5.2 miles east of the Ariel turn-off to an old cabin," Mike said as he returned his cell phone to his belt.

Chief Biskbey had asked Sheriff Grant Taylor to cover the Fleming house and bring in the forensic team. Mike, Karen, Biskbey and another officer had just turned east on Highway 4 at Cathlament when the call from Cooper came in. An officer was driving with Biskbey in the front seat. Karen and Mike were in the back seat. A second Portland police car followed with three deputies.

"I'm going to call Grant and ask him to meet us at the Ariel turnoff," Biskbey said. "We can drop you and Karen off at the Lewis River Inn in Woodland just off Interstate 5."

"You're not about to do that," Karen said. "I'm going to see this through."

"You need rest and your wrists look awful," Mike said.

"They're tender but I'm okay. Let me do it, Mike." She reached for his hand. "Please, Mike, this is mine?"

Biskbey thumbed through a police directory carried in all patrol cars. "Taylor's cell number is here, I hope he answers." He punched the number and turned on the speaker.

"Sheriff Taylor."

"Grant, this is Oran. Cooper just called. The Donovans are in an old cabin 5.2 miles east of the Ariel turnoff. Do you know where that is?"

"I know the area but nothing about an old cabin."

"Why don't we meet at the Ariel turn-off on 503."

"Okay, I'll call four deputies."

"Let's keep it low key, no sirens, not yet anyway."

"Fine, I'm leaving the Fleming house now."

"We're going east on 4, twenty miles west of Longview. It'll take us close to forty minutes, Biskbey said. "I'll call my office and advise the FBI."

"Right," Grant said. "I won't be far behind you."

Biskbey punched in another cell phone number, the number for the officers in the car following behind them. He didn't want to use the police radio—not yet anyway. Then he called his office and instructed them to call Biff Roberts.

≈≈≈≈≈

After meeting at the Ariel turn-off, four police cars continued east 5.2 miles and eased to a stop. Karen, Mike and six officers were huddled on the road when Grant said, "You say we're looking for a gravel drive on the south side of the road?"

"An old obscure gravel drive was Cooper's exact words," Mike said.

"Okay, you guys walk that way and we'll go this way," Grant said. "Give a holler when you find it." Turning to Karen and Mike, "it is sure black out here."

Not near as black as that bag had been, Karen thought. She and Mike waited in the back seat of the patrol car.

"Remember when we used to neck?" Mike said.

"Hmm—you had that old Ford and carried a blanket for nights like this when it was cold." She rested her head on Mike's shoulder. "Hold me close." She nuzzled in his arms and recalled how they had met when they were both seventeen-year-old freshman at San Diego State:

"Is this your first year?" he had said.

She stood just a few feet away. His eyes were brown—his hair dark—almost black—cut flat top. Wearing sandals, she had to look up to him. "I arrived yesterday."

"I'm Mike Dyer."

"Karen Rutterman." She sensed his come-on.

"Have you picked a major?"

"Journalism."

"Me too, may I buy you a Coke?" he said.

She became Karen Dyer in their senior year. How exciting it was when the two of them accepted positions with the Colombia Broadcasting Company in New York City. Mike attended a survival school for six weeks when they began to give him overseas assignments. The curriculum included a study of tactics, hand-to-hand combat, weapons and their modes of operation and intensive training for survival in the midst of terrorist activity. The worst came when he was incarcerated for five days in a mock prison—stripped, hosed down and shackled to a table for two hours. He said he would never forget that. Two years later she requested the same training to be on a par with the men.

"It will be a hostile environment and you will be the only woman." The management at CBS explained. "They won't pull any punches."

"That's okay, I want the training."

The restful period ended when an officer called, "We've found it."

Mike and Karen stepped out of the car. They could see the flashlights three hundred feet ahead.

"They think they found it," Grant called to the officers who had gone the other direction.

Mike, Karen and all the others walked briskly toward the indicated spot.

"It's all grown over with weeds. I'm not sure it was ever a driveway," one of the deputies reported.

"That culvert in the drainage ditch tells us it had been a drive at one time," another said.

"Yeah, try to follow it though," the officer ahead said.

Searching out traces of gravel on the narrow drive, they followed, stepping through dense undergrowth for a hundred feet or more.

"Are you up to this?" Mike said, speaking to Karen.

"You don't really think I'm going to miss this, do you?" *I'm glad I choose loafers instead of heels from that woman's closet.*

"Sorry I asked. Come on, I'll help you."

"I can walk, honey. It's okay."

"There it is!" one of the officers ahead shouted.

When Sheriff Taylor flashed his light from side to side, the vague shape of a cabin could be seen buried in high weeds. The glass panes in an old door above a concrete stoop were gone. The door creaked as it opened. "There's another door a foot or so inside, looks like new plywood," Taylor said. "It has two gate hasps, one on top and one at the bottom with a stick jammed through each of them. A pair of men's shoes and a couple watches are lying here and there's a pocket knife."

Standing behind two other patrolmen she saw Taylor open the plywood door and there was light. "MY GOD," he hollered. "The stench is awful."

The men behind him peered over Taylor's shoulder.

"There's a woman huddled in the corner with a blanket wrapped around her," Taylor reported. As he eased in the two officers peered through the door. "The smell is nauseating."

"No no, don't you touch me," a woman's voice cried out.

Karen and Mike tried to get closer to see but two officers were standing on the old concrete stoop outside the door.

"The man on the floor is dead with a wire wrapped around his neck," Taylor reported.

"Get away from me," the woman said.

"I'm not going to hurt you," Taylor said and then Karen heard him say, "I need some help. Let Mrs. Dyer in."

The two officers backed out and let Karen pass. "Oh no," Karen cried out.

"Yeah, that's what I said," Taylor said glancing back at her. "He's dead and she won't let me touch her."

"It's the Senator."

"I Know." Taylor was standing the double mattress. The Senator lay face up—his dead body filling the floor space between the mattress and the plywood wall.

Foul air permeated Karen's nostrils. She placed her hand over her nose to stifle the odor. Marilyn Donovan, cowered in the far corner at the edge of the mattress in fetal position wrapped in a blanket—her eyes staring—not moving.

Squatting but not moving any closer, Karen said, "I'll see what I can do."

"Stay away from me," Marilyn Donovan pushed back into the corner.

"Mrs. Donovan, I'll get you out of here."

Taylor stepped back to the door. One officer had managed to squeeze in. Another looked over his shoulder.

"Why don't you get out and let me see what I can do with her?"

"Okay, I'll keep an eye on you through the door."

Looking at Marilyn, Karen said, "Come, let me take you out of here."

Marilyn Donovan did not move.

Karen moved a few inches closer and reached toward Marilyn. "I'm not going to hurt you." Their eyes focused on each other. "It's okay. I'll take care of you." Moving closer, Karen reached down and touched her arm. "Come on, let's get out of here."

Marilyn Donovan stood up when Karen tugged on her arm and moved a couple steps toward the door.

"Get the men back. Give her room to pass," Karen said. Then, looking down at Marilyn's feet, "you don't have any shoes. Will you let one of the men carry you?"

"No!"

"Grant, are there any shoes out there?"

"Yeah, one spike heel and a pair of men's shoes."

"That won't help much," she said turning back to Marilyn. "Come on, I'll help you Mrs. Donovan."

When Marilyn Donovan saw the officers grouped outside she buried her face on Karen's shoulder. With Karen's help Marilyn could walk.

"What happened to your husband, Mrs. Donovan?"

"He fell and hit his head after he hit me." She clutched the blanket tight around her body as Karen held her arm to help her through the waist high weeds. "That was my shoe back there."

"Come on, let's go to the car," Mike said.

"I'll have one of my men drive you to the King Hospital in Portland," Biskbey said. "Go get the car," he said to one of the officers."

"I can carry her," Mike said.

"She won't let you touch her."

Biskbey was waiting at the police car with the door open. Karen helped her in and started to close the door when Marilyn screamed, "No."

"I'm not leaving you," Karen said. "I'm going to the other side to get in."

"You're locking me in."

"I'll scoot in beside her," Karen said while still clinging to Marilyn's arm. Mike closed the door and slipped into the front seat. He turned back to face them.

"Who's he?" Marilyn said.

"He's my husband, Mike."

"He plays around, you know."

"No, I don't think so. We love each other."

"They all play around. That's all they think about."

Mike and Karen's eyes met. Neither of them said anything. Turning to Marilyn, Karen said, "what happened to your husband?"

"He went crazy and started bashing his head against the wall. He's dead now!"

"What made him do that?"

"He's just crazy, that's all."

"But you loved him."

"I hated him. He was having sex with every girl in his office and he killed his first wife. He was going to kill me. Can't you understand that?"

"It's okay, I do understand," Karen said pulling her close—hugging her. "Nobody's going to hurt you now."

"Those four men took my watch and left me alone with him."

"You and your husband saw four men?"

"They put a black hood over my head and tied it around my neck. I got sick."

"But they took the hood off."

"No! They left me standing on that mattress with him. That's when I took the hood off."

"And your husband?"

"They took his watch too."

"And the men were gone?"

"Yes."

"Then you never saw the men."

"They were all around me. They took my watch."

"How do you know there were four?"

"I could hear them. One of them was a woman. Why don't you believe me?"

"I do believe you," Karen said pressing Marilyn's head to her shoulder and patting her gently. "It must have been awful."

"It was," Marilyn said laying into Karen's shoulder and wiping her eye with her finger.

"Tell me about it."
"Jay and I were in the parking lot. . . ."

# CLOSING THE OLD CABIN

Sheriff Taylor closed the old cabin knowing that it should remain undisturbed for the forensic team. He waited with Biskbey and four deputies for the FBI. When Biff Roberts and the two FBI agents arrived the urgency was over. A cursory examination and seeing the charger wire snarled around the Senator's neck, made it almost certain that the Senator had been strangled. Taylor wondered about the bruises on the Senator's head.

"The Director sleeping in this morning, Biff?" Biskbey said.

"He wasn't in his room. We left word for him."

The FBI forensic team arrived at the old cabin as the first rays of the sun appeared. Taylor, Biskbey and Biff Roberts returned to the Ariel store. With all the commotion the owner brewed coffee and they were having a second cup when two FBI agents came in.

"They found Bowers," one of the agents said "He's going to stop here before going to the cabin."

"Have some coffee," Grant Taylor said.

"I could go for that."

In just minutes Taylor heard the siren and then, looking through the front window of the Ariel Store he saw a car come to a screeching halt in front of the store. The driver was a young woman. The Director of the FBI was irate as he charged through the door yelling at Biskbey. "You had no business letting that bitch be alone with Donovan's wife."

"You talking about Karen Dyer?" Biskbey said,

The director stood nose to nose glaring at Biskbey. "That slut's been a pain in the ass for years and she'll put this whole thing out on national television. What the hell's the matter with you."

Grant Taylor stepped up. "This may be a federal case but you're in my territory now and Oran Biskbey happens to be my friend."

With no response to Bowers, Taylor turned to Biskbey. "Do you want to do it, or do you want me to do it?"

"Let's do it together."

Biskbey and Taylor grabbed Bowers, one on each side. Biff moved a step closer.

"Stay out of this, Mr. Roberts," Grant Taylor said.

The two FBI agents stood fast. They had heard their director's remarks and Biff wasn't moving.

"What . . . what are you doing?" Bowers said.

"You're in my jurisdiction now," Taylor said. "Let's take a walk."

They were half dragging Bowers between them.

"Let them handle this," Roberts said to the other agents.

Biskbey and Taylor marched the commander and chief out the front door to the parking lot.

"Where are we going?" Bowers said. They stopped and spun him around.

"Bowers, you may be the Chief Honcho in Washington but out here you're in our domain," Biskbey began. "And I don't like what you just said."

"What do you mean?"

"If Karen Dyer is a bitch to you then you're an SOB that needs to be dealt with," Biskbey said, standing nose to nose with Bowers.

"I want you out of here within the next five minutes," Taylor said.

"You can't tell me what to do. This is a federal case."

Taylor moved around in front to grab Bowers by the front of his shirt. "Your men can stay but you gotta go."

"You can't make me go."

"Oh, yes I can. If I tossed you in that river right now, nobody would stop me. Look around, Bowers, count your friends. Taylor released his shirt. "Now you get out of here."

Biskbey and Taylor left him standing alone and returned to the store.

"Your boss is going to speak a lot softer from now on, Mr. Roberts," Taylor said.

Bowers came in and went straight to Biff. "I need to get back to Washington. You can clean things up here."

"Yeah, we can do that," Biff said.

Biskbey couldn't resist a last strike. "Maybe you should leave your plane for your men."

Bowers looked at Biskbey and then at Sheriff Taylor. "Yeah, good idea. I'll take the airline."

~~~~~

At Olympia, Washington a few miles west of Tacoma, Ted Bolan pulled off the freeway and drove a short distance to a bridge. He looked at his Browning, one of two that he had carried in the CIA for thirty years. He tossed it into the deep water and then returned to his van to drive two miles to a second bridge to toss the New York cellular phone. *I'll destroy Old Granny first thing in the morning.* By the time he arrived home it was past 2 o'clock. The bedroom light was on. Molly met him at the door. "Are you all right?"

"Yes, of course." He opened the screen door.

"Don't say that . . . I'm not happy with you." She moved aside.

"I guess you saw it all on TV." He reached for her hand and she pulled it back.

"That was ten hours ago!" She let him kiss her with no response when his fingers curled around her neck to press his cheek to her cheek. "Where have you been?"

"It's a long story." He eased his hold on her neck. "I'm kind of hungry."

"Come into the kitchen."

# It's Going to Come Out

On Friday morning, after they left Marilyn at the hospital, the clock on the bedside table read 3:38 when Mike and Karen arrived at their room in the Lewis River Inn. Biff and the FBI staff were staying at the same motel. Seven hours later the phone rang. Mike answered. It was Biff.

"How is Mrs. Donovan?"

"We didn't stay at the hospital long. They were taking her to a room as we left. A police officer had been assigned to stand guard."

"Yeah, Biskbey said he was going to do assign a guard. It's a good idea. How about joining us for a brunch at eleven," Biff said. "I'll knock on your door. The restaurant is across the street."

"Wanna have brunch with Biff at eleven, honey?"

"Fine," Karen said.

"Sounds good, Biff. We'll be ready."

"Also, we have to get Karen's side of the story before you fly back to New York. Can you come to Judy Loche's office after brunch."

Judy Loche was the director of the FBI field office in Portland, the same position Biff held in New York.

"Karen's been through quite a lot Biff," Mike said.

"Judy Loche wanted to do it this morning but went along with pushing it back to one thirty."

"I'm sure Karen'll want to clear everything up before returning to New York. Her show will be full of it on Monday morning."

"I'm sure it will. We'll fly back right after the meeting with Judy Loche. I assume you are coming with us."

"Yes, we'll do that. See you at eleven." As Mike hung up he saw his wife at the mirror. "Judy Loche wants to talk with you this afternoon at 1:30 in her office." He wondered about the clothes she was wearing. "Where did you change clothes?"

"Mike, I put these clothes on at the Fleming house because those men tied my hands to a beam. Barstelli cut every stitch of clothing from my body. I didn't want to tell you that part."

He came to her and held her close as she sobbed, telling him everything—the way they abducted her—the body bag—the old garage and then the ride to the Fleming house. "I was still naked when Cooper found me and shot Barstelli. I shot one of those men with Barstelli's gun."

≈≈≈≈≈

"How are you feeling?" Biskbey said, speaking to Karen as she, Mike and Biff slipped into a booth at the restaurant.

"I'm okay."

"Those bruises on your wrists look tender," Biskbey said.

"They are."

"They're going to ask you about it this afternoon," Biff said.

"Yes, I suppose they will."

"Are there things you'd rather not tell?" Biff said.

Their eyes met. "Biff there are a lot of things I don't want to talk about and I'd just as soon drop the subject."

"Any new developments?" Mike said, looking at Biskbey.

"We found the old green Ford," Biskbey said. Turning to Karen, he added, "It was parked off the road in the brush not more than a half mile from where he told us to wait."

"Just around that bend in the road?" Karen said.

"That's right."

"Oran, that man with the bib overalls and the old lady manikin was him," Karen said.

"I think so. He had the old station wagon parked there ready to go."

"We drove up that road. How did we miss seeing the old Ford?"

"He drove it into the brush fifty feet or more and it was getting dark. We found that old station wagon he was driving parked in the casino parking lot in La Center across the street from Dewey's Hardware. A man purchased both cars yesterday. The name he gave for the old green Ford was Leonard Gibbons. The old wagon was purchased about two hours later from Al's Wrecking Yard by . . . " he looked at his notes, "a Gabriel Pearson. Neither address checked out."

"You're sure the same man bought both of them?" Mike asked.

"Yeah," Biskbey said. "Dark complexion, Hispanic maybe, fifty or sixty years old, baseball cap, the same man Miss Dyer and I saw in the old wagon with the manikin."

"Chief, we've spent enough time together. Why don't you start calling me Karen?"

"We did get to know each other, didn't we?" Biskbey said scratching his cheek.

"Yes we did. I wonder what he did with the old manikin."

"The car was wiped clean. The manikin of the old woman was a clever ploy to get past us. I sure thought he was old Rufus."

"And there was nothing in either of the cars?" Mike asked.

"They're going over them now. Both cars looked as though they had been cleaned out and there were no prints on the steering wheel or door handles."

"He was wearing gloves," Karen reminded him.

"Not in the old station wagon, he wasn't. I saw his hands," Biskbey said.

"Now wait a minute," Biff said. "Let's recap what we know."

"Yeah, let's do that, Biff," Karen said. "We know that three or four men abducted the Donovans and that a man wearing a hood risked his life to save me."

Biff laughed. "Yeah, I guess that's about it."

# KAREN TELLS ALL

At fifty-five, Judy Loche could still turn a man's eye. A successful attorney for many years, divorced twice, she had been with the FBI for the last three years. "I've been an admirer of yours for many years, Mrs. Dyer. How nice to meet you," she said in the outer office.

"Nice to meet you too."

"We'll use the conference room."

"Can Mike come with me?"

"Yes, of course." Judy Loche said gesturing to an open door. Most celebrities are disappointing when you meet them up close but not Karen Dyer, she thought. *Her features and mannerisms are striking—be fun to go to bed with her.*

Biff and three other officers were already seated at a table. They all rose. Karen and Mike took two of several vacant chairs at the table. Judy Loche took her place at the head of the table. A recording secretary followed with a pad in hand and took the chair to Judy Loche's left. A tape recorder sat on the table.

Judy Loche introduced the other officers and then asked, "Why don't you begin with the time when you and Chief Biskbey arrived at the Federal Bank.

Karen told them about her abduction at the Chevron station, the body bag and Cooper's phone call. She told them about Bastelli and hearing the names Marchak, Angelli and Lewiski in the old garage and the way they tied her hand and foot before putting her in that body bag. She told them about the conversation she heard in the back of the car and the shooting spree when D. B. Cooper rescued her.

"What did Mrs. Donovan tell you last night about what happened to them?"

"She and the Senator were abducted by three or four men—one of them may have been a woman. After putting hoods over their heads they forced them into a van and took them to that old cabin and left them alone. She said the Senator bashed his head against the wall."

"One of the officers said you have some mean looking bruises on your wrists,".

They tied my wrists and ankles, Karen pushed the jacket sleeves up and unbuttoned both cuffs. The outline of the cords was clearly visible at the small of her wrists.

"They must have tied you tight to cause bruises like that," Judy Loche said.

"Yes, they're still tender."

"You were wearing a suit with a skirt when they abducted you." Judy Loche said.

"Yes."

"And you were wearing slacks when they found you last night."

Karen turned to Mike as she buttoned the cuffs and pulled her jacket sleeves down over her wrists. Then, looking at Judy Loche, "I didn't want to tell that part." She glanced around the table. They waited in silence. "They strung me up to a beam in a cold empty garage and cut every stitch of clothing from my body. That's how I got the bruises. They put me in that body bag and took me to the house where you found me. I was still naked when D. B. Cooper found me. He sent me into the house to find these clothes."

The room fell silent. Judy Loche broke the trance. "Then you were naked when the shooting took place."

"Cooper loaned me his parka."

"And you don't think he was in on it?"

"No."

"How did he find you?"

"He called me on the phone that had been taken from locker 102 in New York City and talked to Barstelli. Beyond that, I don't know how he found me. I do know that he would have died for me."

"Didn't he say anything that might give us a clue as to who he is?"

"No, he didn't."

"Can you remember anything that might help us to find that old garage?"

"I was in that body bag when they carried me in and when they carried me out. The door was open and headlights provided the light."

"I think we've heard enough," Biff said.

"Yes, I think we have," Judy Loche said. "There is one last question which I have to ask, Mrs. Dyer."

Karen turned and stared straight at her.

"Did they molest you?"

"Not sexually."

"And you haven't seen a doctor?"

"No."

Speaking to Biff and the others at the table, Judy Loche said, "We have to find that garage."

"That won't be difficult, now that we have the two men and know the right questions to ask," one of the officers said. "We already have enough to get indictments against Lewiski, Marchak and Angelli."

# HE SAVED ME

On the return FBI flight to New York City, Mike and Karen took seats near the back of the plane away from the others. Biff had helped with that arrangement to give them the privacy they wanted. Karen looked at her watch. It had been an hour since they left Judy Loche's office. She knew Mike was thinking about Cooper and her abduction.

"How do you think he found you?"

"I don't know, Mike."

"He must have known something."

She looked at her husband. "Mike, he would never have let them to do those things to me."

"He had to know."

"No . . . no, Mike. He didn't." She stared straight at him. *How can I make him understand?*

"What did he do to create such an impression on you?"

She placed her hand on his face and pressed his cheek to hers. "Honey, he came for me. Somehow he figured out where I was, I don't know how but he did. He would have given his life to save me. He's a man who knew exactly what he was doing. He's smart, Mike."

"He must be a hell of a man."

"He is." Karen kissed her husband on the cheek. "He said he met you one time and saw me at a Rotary meeting many years ago."

"If he's the real D. B. Cooper, he's past seventy."
Suddenly she knew. She pushed away.
"What's wrong? What did I say?"
She remembered. D. B. Cooper did it all alone in 1971 and they never found a trace of him. Then, staring into Mike's eyes, "he didn't have a gang. He did it all alone."
"His men were watching everything on television. The Donovans said there were three, maybe four."
"He's a man of many voices. He fooled all of us. I saw him in action. He did the whole thing by himself—it couldn't be any other way. Cooper knew we'd figure that out. The NEWDAY Show is going to scoop everybody Monday morning."
"Are you sure? You don't think he had men watching?"
"The whole thing was a spoof." She laid her head on his shoulder.
"You're proposing that we air this without confirmation?"
"Honey, we have confirmation, I was there—it can't be any other way. There weren't any other men."
"We have to be sure."
Her head rested easy under his chin, relaxed, her dilemma had been solved. D. B. Cooper would be a hero again, a lone bandit to enchant the world. "Honey, there's no way three men could have gotten in that small box the way Marilyn Donovan said they did. He did it all by himself. I know he did. Think about it. He bought the old cars. We know enough to reconstruct the whole sequence of events, his planning, everything."
"But we don't know who he is," he said.
"On Monday morning we'll give the public a complete rundown starting with a lone hijacker in 1971. We'll renew the folktale. The World Trade Center Fund will not only keep the Senator's money but the contributions will pour in just the way he said they would."
"And you know all this just from having been with him last night?"

"Mike, he knows things. He made Lewiski tell about the way Carol Fleming distributed money for Barstelli to Roger Stark, Bowers and Donovan."

"Carol Fleming?"

"Honey, there are so many things I need to tell you and follow-up on. We watched him work yesterday afternoon. He had every detail planned. He's sharp, Mike."

"And you like him."

"Oh, yes."

"But you don't know who he is or how he found you."

"Honey, he's a man of many talents and I hope we never find out. I know that he offered $300,000 to them and that all the shooting started a half hour after those two men arrived. Maybe he followed them. We just don't know. If D. B. Cooper is as good as I think he is, we'll never know. I can tell everything I know Monday morning to scoop all the networks and it won't hurt him a bit. He knew we'd figure it out."

≈≈≈≈≈

The plush light blue carpet added elegance to the reception lobby of the law firm of Stark, Holman, Jackson & Associates. Historic pictures in polished black frames of old New York beside current pictures taken from the same vantage point were mounted at eye level down a long hall leading to many offices.

Roger Stark's office was a corner room with two tinted glass walls facing north and east. He was the only person around on this Sunday morning. The phone was tight to his ear. "Hell, the money's clean," he heard Bowers say. "Nothing bigger than a twenty. He can spend it any place."

"But you stopped that check?"

"Not exactly. Cooper demanded that the check be deposited at the Federal Bank and then to the World Trade Center Relief Fund."

"You had all day Friday to stop that check"

"They won't release it without a court order and that has to come from the Senator and he's dead. You're the executor of his estate, can't you do something?"

"We'll get to that first thing Monday morning. I want that money deposited in my account." Stark said.

"Don't be too sure. There are a lot of people throughout the country who didn't like the Senator. D. B. Cooper's a folk hero and the sentiment toward helping the Trade Center victims is strong."

"Oh, hell, you're the Director. Cooper stole that money and killed the Senator."

"Public opinion is going Cooper's way. He did it all on national television so we couldn't move in on him."

"His gang committed a crime and killed the Senator. He's a terrorist. We gotta play that up, really smear him. Is Dyer going to do her show Monday?"

"Far as I know."

"Where do her loyalties lie?" Stark said.

"She claims Cooper saved her life."

"What happened to the Senator?"

"Cooper's men killed him."

# THE CONFESSION

Judy Loche and two agents arrived at the King Hospital a few minutes after nine o'clock on Sunday morning. She had wanted to see Marilyn Donovan on Saturday but the doctor said she was too sedated.

Marilyn Donovan was sitting in a chair when Judy Loche and the two agents entered her room. She sat down in a chair facing Marilyn. Two agents stood off to the side.

"How are you feeling?" Judy Loche began.

"I'm all right. The doctor said I could return to Washington this afternoon."

"You look all right."

"I'm fine. They've been nice to me here."

"You know why we're here?"

"The doctor said you wanted to ask me some questions."

"Yes, there are some details we need to clear up. We found your watch, earrings and necklace outside of that old cabin where they found you."

"Those men made me take them off. It was awful."

"Miss Dyer said that you told her that your husband bashed his head against the wall and killed himself," Judy Loche said.

"Yes, that's what he did."

"But there was a cord wrapped around his neck. We think he was strangled."

Marilyn Donovan looked away, then down at the floor. "I wouldn't know about that."

"It's going to come out in the autopsy report. We're sure he was strangled."

Marilyn turned back quick—looking straight at Judy Loche. "Cooper and his men did it!"

"But you said they left you with a hood over your head and you never saw them."

"I don't know how they did it."

"You told Mrs. Dyer that your husband beat you."

"Yes, that's what he did, he beat me." Marilyn Donovan stared at the floor again.

"And you killed him in self-defense."

Leaning forward, her face buried in her hands, she cried out. "Yes, yes, I killed him!"

Never looking up, her face in her hands, she blurted it out. "He was lying there on his back, that fat old man. I hated him. I ask him if he wanted a root beer. . ."

She told Judy Loche about the massage and the way she turned his head to strike with the coke can and then three times around his neck with the cell phone cord.

"Then you did it on purpose," Judy Loche said

"Yes, yes! He beat me and he was having sex with all the girls in the office. I hated him. You know he killed his first wife."

"How do you know that?"

"Everybody knows it."

≈≈≈≈≈

Mike and Karen slept in later than usual on Sunday morning—lying close—their bodies entwined.

"Mike, I've been thinking about it. I didn't want anybody to know about it, not even you—especially you. But like we both learned in Judy Loche's office, there's no way I can stop it from coming out. The networks already know the story anyway—except the details. I'm going to tell everything."

"Are you sure you want to do this?"

"Honey, we can't stop it."

"What can you say that you didn't already tell us in Judy Loche's office."

"Ooh," She eased away and looked into Mike's eyes. "There are many things that nobody else knows and I know how to put the color in it. Our ratings will soar and the World Trade Center Victims Fund will keep the money. Stark won't be able to do anything. He'll have to jump on the bandwagon just to make himself look good."

# THE STORY GOES OUT

The set for the NEWDAY Show had two areas. One area had a fireplace with expensive furniture that could be arranged to suit the mood of the script. The second area had a console that could seat four people. Banks of monitors behind glass and many technicians were in the dark areas surrounding the two sets.

Bill Lubsky, the night managing editor, saw Karen Dyer coming. She was late. It was after five. He was surprised to see her accompanied by Mike. He didn't generally come in until eight.

"Morning Bill," she said. "Got a minute?"

He followed them into her office. Her hair cascaded over her shoulders the way he liked to see it—the way she wore it most all the time. A trench coat hung open in front exposing a skirt that ended above her knees.

"See you later honey," Mike said as he started for the door. "Anything I need to know, Bill?"

"No, nothing out of the ordinary, " Bill Lubsky said. "The night's been quiet. I'll drop by your office before I go home."

"Good." Mike disappeared down the hall.

Karen hung her trench coat on a hall tree in one corner of her office and sat down behind her desk. Bill took a chair in front.

"I'll start my monologue seated at the console. I don't need anything special."

"That's it."

"That's all."

Bill Lubsky left her office. He had expected a more explosive production on the Monday following her abduction.

At two minutes before seven Bill watched Karen come out and review the set without comment. She's lovely, he thought. She always is. She took her seat behind the console and acknowledged the newscaster to her right. She waited. In sixty seconds she'd be on the air.

Glancing at the prompter, Bill Lubsky noted that her opening segment was short—only three sentences. He was surprised when he saw Mike standing in a darkened area of the set.

"I thought I'd catch her show live this morning," Mike said.

"Yeah, me too."

The countdown ended and she began: "Good morning ladies and gentlemen. Welcome to NEWDAY on this Monday morning. Today I will tell you the story about D. B. Cooper and the way a man named Rostel Barstelli and his men abducted me but first, the news." The camera shifted to the newscaster seated to Karen's right.

"Our lead story today is D. B. Cooper," the commentator began. "He has disappeared with no trace just as he did thirty years ago, if he is indeed the same man. He is reported to be a man . . ."

As the news continued Karen returned to her office. Bill and Mike watched as the commentator reported the details of Karen Dyer's rescue. Pictures were shown of Barstelli's and Carol Fleming's bodies covered with a sheet. A camera panned the vehicles to show the flat tires before focusing on another covered body and then the pool of blood where the man had laid near the open garage door. "The FBI has confirmed that . . . ."

At the end of the news segment, during the commercial break, Karen returned to her seat behind the console. She made final adjustments to her attire and checked the earbob and lapel mike buried in her hair. She looked at the technician. "Okay?"

He gave her a thumbs-up. The countdown started. "5—4—3—2—1."

"Ladies and Gentlemen, after my rescue from racketeer Rostel Barstelli and his men I wanted to hide everything and tell you as little as possible. Then the questions from the FBI and the media made it apparent to me and then to my husband, that the full story must be told—there was no way to keep it quiet. It's the kind of a story a woman does not like to tell, or, in my case, admit to."

Bill Lubsky listened, hanging on every word.

"The crimes that were committed must be brought to light and presented in their true perspective for all to know and evaluate. These crimes were not of my doing, or something that I should be ashamed of, or punished for. Those men were the perpetrators and they are the ones who should be punished. This morning you are going to hear the story exactly the way it happened.

"Last Thursday in Portland Oregon, after a man who claimed to be D. B. Cooper deposited a twenty-five million dollar check and took $300,000 in cash, a group of men brutally abducted me. They grabbed me and clamped a rag soaked with chloroform over my face. These men were Rostel Barstelli's henchmen, the man who fled the country just eight months ago when warrants were issued for his arrest."

Bill Lubsky listened as she told her story about regaining consciousness in a body bag and the first phone call from D. B. Cooper and then the opening of that bag and staring up at those rafters with six men staring down on her. Mike stood twenty feet away.

## D.B. Cooper -aftermath-

"They lifted me to my feet. I was facing Barstelli when he saw the phone that Cooper had called me on. Then Barstelli spotted the lapel mike with the wire running under my blouse and ordered his men to strip me. They made me stand with my wrists tied to a beam while Barstelli cut and ripped every stitch of clothing from my body."

Bill Lubsky glanced around the set. Mike had moved a few steps closer. Every eye was on her as she told her story about riding nude in a body bag in the back seat of a car strapped in while Barstelli and Lewiski discussed killing her or taking her to South America as a pawn to get his drug associates released, then arriving at Carol Fleming's house and finally the electrifying rescue by Cooper and the way she shot a man who was about to shoot him.

"He sent me into that house to find some clothes. When I came out of the house dressed, ladies and gentlemen, he said something most unusual: 'I liked the view better before.' It wasn't a snide remark, he meant it. He had a way of being fresh and making a woman like it. He then asked me if I knew my husband's cell phone number and handed me a phone. Mike answered on the first ring. Ladies and gentlemen there aren't words to describe how good he sounded.

"With that, this man who called himself D. B. Cooper walked into the darkness. In just thirty minutes I was in my husband's arms."

≈≈≈≈≈

Damn that woman, Roger Stark thought as he flipped the TV off. She has the whole country stirred up. By the time he reached his office at Stark, Holman and Jackson, his two partners were waiting for him. "You know what's going to happen?" Holman said.

"Yeah, I know exactly what's going to happen," Stark said.

"Every Tom, Dick and Harry will be sending money to the World Trade Relief Fund," Jackson chimed in. "There's no way we can demand the return of that twenty-five million."

"Yeah, the best thing we can do is to formally award the money. The public will at least applaud us for doing that," Stark said.

"What are we going to do about Donovan's wife?" Holman questioned.

"Nothing," Roger Stark said. "Donovan probably did attack her. All we can do is represent her. I don't think she'll be indicted."

"What about Donovan's money?" Holman questioned. "He had her excluded in the trust."

"Yeah but that won't fly now. She'll have us in court for the next ten years," Stark said.

"How much?"

"Five million, maybe."

# Molly Remembers

Ted and Molly sat at the breakfast table overlooking the water two hundred feet below. They could see the ships passing by. The TV was on. Karen Dyer had just closed her program on this Monday morning.

"Is that the way it happened?" Molly said picking up her cup and peering over the rim at her husband.

"She described it pretty well." Ted just sat there, not moving—he hadn't even finished his coffee.

"That's a terrible thing for a woman to go through."

"I didn't plan that part of it."

"How did you learn she was in trouble?"

Ted told her about the dark deserted ball field, jumping into the pickup, the convenience store and then his version of the shoot out.

"You could have been killed!"

"It was kind of touch and go for a while." He reached for his cup.

"But you didn't leave her?"

"No, of course not—and you would not have wanted me to."

*No, he is not that kind of a man.* "I hope this is the last of your capers."

"Yes, this is the last."

For now, she thought. "What are you going to do with the $300,000?"

"We're going to spend it."

"I'll have to get used to paying cash for everything again."

"It's all safe money. They don't have the first serial number. Don't make any large expenditures—nothing over two hundred dollars."

Hmn, she smiled as she remembered that 'D. B. Cooper Day' was less than a month away on the Saturday following Thanksgiving. "Are we going to the D. B. Cooper celebration?" Molly said.

"Of course, we always go. All our friends are expecting us."

"I know but you have aroused everybody and there will be a lot more media coverage this year. Every cop in the country will be there." She saw the corners of his mouth turn up as that boyish grin appeared. *He's just a kid and he's fun but I wish he'd behave.*

"We'd be conspicuous by our absence," he said.

"I suppose so." Looking back, it was like re-living an adventure—remembering the part that she would never tell: On their first trip from Ariel, Washington to New York City in January 1972 they had just over $190,000—all twenties.

"We'll carry it in a brief case," he had said.

"And what if they search?"

"They're not going to search. It's not bulky and only weighs fifteen pounds. They have no reason to search."

"Maybe we should check it through."

"It would have our name on it. We'll carry it with us."

Now, thirty years later, she recalled that he had been right. They had passed through security just as he said they would. *I had only known him two months before our move to New York City.* She was Molly Spencer then and lived in her uncle's house just two miles from Ariel. She had agreed to take care of his golden retriever while he and his wife vacationed in Europe. They wouldn't come home until January. She had quit a boring job in Seattle to help them out.

Molly had been alone on that Thanksgiving Day in 1971 when she saw him for the first time. The dog's barking brought her out onto the back porch. There he sat, on the ground with his back against the old storage building fifty feet away, looking at the dog and then at her.

"What are you doing here?" She called moving to the top of the steps.

"I need help," he said.

*A beggar no doubt.* She stepped down off the porch but stopped and turned back.

"No, please, I'm hurt."

The dog trotted to him. The man seemed harmless.

"I think I've broken my ankle," he said.

"How did you get here?" She moved a few steps in his direction.

"I was hiking late yesterday afternoon when I fell. I've been trying to get to the road all night."

Molly moved to the concrete slab at the foot of the steps. He was wearing hiking clothes. "May I look at your ankle?"

"Please do."

He winced in pain when she slipped the boot off and felt around the foot and ankle. "I don't think it's broken. It feels to me like you may have strained the tendons. It's swollen. You need to see a doctor."

"No, just let me rest for a few hours. Do you have something to eat? I can pay you."

"I'll help you into the house and get you something." With her help, he could walk. She cooked bacon and eggs with hash browns as they shared their first breakfast. He was an educated man with good manners. "What's your name?"

"Rick Pullman—and yours?"

"Molly Spencer." She liked him. It would be nice to have someone to spend Thanksgiving with—she had never liked being alone. She made him comfortable in the living room and settled down in one of the overstuffed chairs across from him. "Where's your home?"

"Tacoma."

"What brings you to this part of the country?"

"It's a good area for hunting, fishing and hiking. I know the area well."

"Alone?"

"Yeah . . . this time." He looked around the room. "You have a nice home."

"It belongs to my uncle and his wife. I'm dog-sitting while they're in Europe."

As they talked, she felt the need to prepare a Thanksgiving dinner for him but didn't know why, having known him for only a few hours. She went to the store to buy groceries. He was asleep when she returned.

An airline hijacking was the only news that Thanksgiving Day. The lone hijacker had totally confused the authorities. They knew he disappeared somewhere between Seattle and Reno. There was speculation that he may not have jumped at all, that he exited through the rear stairs after landing in Reno as the plane turned off the runway.

The aroma from the kitchen drifted through the house as Molly went to her vanity to freshen her makeup. She put on hose and slipped into a new dress—the one with the short skirt. He was awake when she strolled into the living room.

As they shared dinner, talked and listened to the news, she became suspicious. By late afternoon she became convinced that this man with the injured ankle was indeed the culprit. It all fit. The way he was dressed, his injury, yes, it all fit. She blurted it out: "Are you D. B. Cooper?"

He had hesitated and then rose to his feet. "I need to be excused."

He hobbled toward the bathroom. As the minutes passed she began to wonder if he might have slipped away through the window. The bathroom window was small and high off the floor and even higher above the ground. Could he have done it? She wished she hadn't said anything and hoped he hadn't gone. Then the door opened and he limped back into the living room. He looked straight at her.

"You guessed right." He explained the details about negotiating with the airlines and then jumping out.

By Friday morning he could walk with a cane. He took her to the spot where he had landed and recovered the parachute and a business suit hidden in a hollow tree. "What's with the suit?" She asked.

"I was wearing it."

"You changed clothes?"

"No, I wore it over the hiking clothes."

"Why?"

"If you want to blend with the crowd you don't get on airplanes in hiking clothes."

The news had reported D. B. Cooper to be heavyset. *Rick Pullman had the build of a trim athlete but wearing a suit over hiking clothes, he would have looked heavy.* "Where's the money?"

"After hiding the clothes, I followed the creek, just as we did today. I carried the money for an hour or more but the pain in my ankle was too severe to continue with all that weight. I stashed it between two large trees under some brush. I think I saw the spot as we went by. You saw me stop a while ago."

"I saw you stop but you didn't say anything about the money."

"I wasn't sure and I've looked continuously as we've walked. I know I stayed close to the creek. Let's work our way back to those two trees. I buried it under some brush."

*It was pitch black last night. How could he have seen anything?* "What does it look like?"

"A new olive drab canvas bag, the kind banks use to transport money."

The frantic search began with Ted resting frequently. "You're ankle's hurting?"

"Yeah—maybe the money is downstream."

"I'll walk a ways and see what I can find," she had said.

When Molly spotted the canvas bag it was open and half under water. When she reached for it, she slipped and hung onto the dense foliage along the creek's bank in knee high water. The top portion of the canvas bag had been gnawed away. She tried to lift it from the water while grabbing bundles of banded money to keep them from floating away. Struggling, holding the bag tight against her body, she made her way to the top of the creek bank and returned to where she had left him.

He grabbed the bag and began examining it. It didn't look new anymore. "It's wet and soaked." He saw remnants of candy wrappers. "I slipped six candy bars from the galley into the bag before I jumped. Some of the money may have floated away after the animals drug the bag to the creek bank."

Molly touched the gnawed flap. "The animals must have been after the candy," she said. She reached down to examine the bag. She returned to the place where she found the canvas bag but saw no money. Then she walked downstream for a quarter mile or more. Nothing.

"It could have floated for miles," she said upon her return.

"Yes, it could have."

They returned home and burned both parachutes and the suit in the fireplace. They dried and counted the money, $178,620.

Molly's life before D. B. Cooper, from the time she was a child, had been plain and ordinary. "Don't take chances, be careful," her mother had repeated day after day. Since that Thanksgiving Day in 1971 her life had stopped being ordinary. She couldn't pinpoint exactly when she fell in love with him.

Smiling, she remembered the way her skirt had slipped up just a bit that first day but she didn't pull it down. *He was in my bedroom by Saturday night.*

*D.B. Cooper -aftermath-*

A week after the hijacking, Ted told her that his real name was Ted Bolan. He had divorced his wife and gave her everything. He was broke. That and the fact that he knew how to do it, created the motivation for the hijacking.

The search in southwestern Washington had grown intense. The authorities did not figure out where he jumped for two weeks.

Ted had taken a leave-of-absence from the CIA and it was time to return to New York. They were together. *I had a new beginning with an exciting man.*

Their first problem had been the money. Yes, they had $178,620 but could they spend it? They knew the FBI had listed the serial numbers. The news had reported that. Ted pointed out that they could spend a few dollars at a time to buy groceries and pay rent but no large amounts. He explained how to accumulate safe money. Break twenties and keep the tens, fives and ones. It was hard the first few times. Molly was sure everybody was watching—that every cash register had a list of serial numbers taped to it. This of course wasn't so, three thousand miles away from the crime scene, weeks and then months later. Ted warned her many times not to become careless and to use safe money when in doubt. She had to get used to carrying several hundred dollars in her purse.

Molly enjoyed those memories. Her first New York driver's license had a picture with a radiance that she'd never seen in herself before. For the first time in her life she thought of herself as pretty—not the plain Jane her family had alluded to. When Ted took her in his arms he loved her and she loved him.

Ted was gone a great deal of the time and Molly got a job as a typist and soon promoted to bookkeeper. She became the owner's private secretary within six months.

After Ted retired from the CIA they returned to Tacoma and bought the hundred-year-old-house overlooking Puget Sound. Seeing Ted looking out over the Sound, Molly sighed. The world needs to know the full story, to know this man as

*Gene Elmore*

she does, his secrets—she would start writing something to leave behind.

# The Noose Closes

The FBI asked Karen and Chief Biskbey about the time they saw Cooper in the station wagon without the felt hood.

"It was dark and he had a dark complexion," they both confirmed. The Moreland Motel and the two people from whom he purchased the cars provided the same description.

Also, Karen saw the report about the man whose car Cooper commandeered to take him to Longview just minutes after he left her. Cooper was wearing his hood then.

Contributions poured in and the World Trade Center Fund pushing it to more than a fifty million. "Even the young people applauded him," Karen said.

≈≈≈≈≈

Karen pulled the file on Pauline Donovan's death. An excerpt from Dr. Tina Mathews's Autopsy Report read:

> When a person drowns they struggle for breath. It's a horrible death. The lung cells become twice as large. The cells taken from Mrs. Donovan's lungs were not enlarged and they are positive proof that she did not drown. Also, she was found floating in the pool. She was not a fat person and her body would have sunk to the bottom if the lungs had been full of water.

X rays document a fractured skull and a resulting clot. Pauline Donovan died from a blow to the head with a blunt instrument. She was dead before her body entered the water.

Karen was puzzled as to why, with such a positive report, Pauline Donovan's death could have been ruled accidental. Reading further in the file she learned that a Dr. Duane Gordon quit his position as Los Angeles County coroner a decade before. He did quite well at many trials as an expert witness. His fee was never less than $25,000. In this case, the fee had been $100,000 plus expenses.

Reading from the transcript—his testimony at the inquest:

"Dr. Gordon, how long did you serve as the chief pathologist at Cook Claremont Hospital in Los Angeles?"

"Nineteen years, sir."

And in that time, Doctor, how many drowning victims were you called upon to examine?"

"Too many, I'm sorry to say. The beaches in LA are extremely active and crowded with surfers and swimmers. In my tenure, I examined more than two hundred and fifty drownings."

"So it is no exaggeration to say that this is an area in which you have a level of expertise?"

"I have examined more drowning victims than any pathologist in the world."

"How do you explain the condition of the body, Dr. Gordon? Pictures taken of the deceased show a fractured skull indicating that she died from a blow to the head."

"It's not uncommon for swimmers to strike the bottom of a pool. Sometimes they hit hard enough break their necks. In Mrs. Donovan's case, the fracture occurred at the top of the head just to the left of center above the forehead."

"As you know, I asked you to bring pictures of other victims to illustrate this point. Will you share those with the court, Dr. Gordon?"

"One of these is a young boy and the other is a woman just about the same age as Mrs. Donovan. Both have fractured skulls very similar to Mrs. Donovan's."

"Is there anything else you found that could shed light on her death?"

"The autopsy revealed significant amounts of marijuana in her bloodstream, as if she had inhaled one or perhaps two marijuana cigarettes."

"Why would that be relevant, Dr. Gordon?"

"Marijuana impairs a person's judgment and they become bolder. This is probably the reason she struck the bottom."

"Thank you, Dr. Gordon. I have no further questions."

Reading on, Karen read the transcript of Dr. Tina Mathews' testimony:

"I am a pathologist for the Washington Hospital Center and the chief medical examiner in Washington D. C."

"So, unlike Dr. Gordon, you actually examined Pauline Donovan's body?"

"Yes."

"How many hours did you devote to her examination?"

"Fifty-three."

"Is that more than usual?"

"Sometimes. In this case I was convinced that her death was not an accident."

"What evidence did you consider?"

"In addition to an extensive physical examination of the corpse, I took multiple X-rays. I sampled and compared lung tissue."

"And according to your report, which I have here, you concluded that Mrs. Donovan died from a blow to the head and that she died before entering the water. Is that correct?"

"Those were my findings. However, upon further consideration and soul searching and the benefit of Dr. Gordon's extensive experience, I've concluded that those initial findings were incorrect, that the evidence does point toward drowning."

≈≈≈≈

Andrew Phillips was clean-shaven with white hair cropped short. Karen knew he had just turned sixty. Sitting across the table he looked quite distinguished even in his prison garb. Two cameras were in place, one viewing Karen, the other focused on Phillips. Each camera had an operator. Two guards stood off to the side.

Karen and Phillips had already exchanged pleasantries and parlayed a few questions. He didn't deny anything, he had killed eight people, it was a part of his record.

"Did you ever meet Dr. Tina Mathews?" Karen said.

He smiled. "The Senator's dead now. I'll tell you the story, Miss Dyer. It was an early Monday morning in July 1991 when I parked a block down the street from a modest house in Hyattsville, Maryland. The night air was hot and sultry.

"Things were getting tight. The inquest concerning Pauline Donovan's death was just two days away. Tina Mathews' written report had to be squelched. Killing her was not the answer. She'd have to testify. My orders were: *Do what I had to do.*

"On that night, her husband was in Hutchinson, Kansas. She'd only been married three weeks. I recall that colorful flowers were in bloom on the porch and the roof on a single car detached garage had seen better days. An aging mailbox had *Mathews* freshly painted across in white script. For that little slice of paradise, the doctor spent fourteen hours a day elbow deep in stiffs, coming up with creative theories about how they got that way. Her civic-mindedness baffled me. With her looks she could have been pulling a million per in New York.

"I knew the doc's loyal pooch was a lover, no problem there. I pulled a stocking down over my face and quietly let myself in. The dog met me at the door. I squatted and rubbed the dog's ears gently and slipped him a fresh ham bone before going up the stairs toward Tina Mathews' bedroom. The door was open. She lay on top of the sheets in her bra and panties sleeping with just a wisp of a snore. The dog's smarter than she is, I thought.

He stayed downstairs in the coolest part of the house. I assume you've seen pictures of Tina Mathews."

"No I haven't," Karen said.

"She was quite nice. I placed my flashlight on the dresser to illuminate the area before sitting down next to her on the bed and watched her breathe. She slept soundly until I slipped my hand between her legs and that got her up fast, all full of piss and vinegar.

"She yelled at me and pulled away, raising her hands to fight. She saw my hooded face and the gun with the silencer attached to a long barrel coming at her. I pushed the hard steel barrel into her chin forcing her head back.

"You're a smart woman, a doctor, I said to her. You know what this is about, don't you?

"She shook her head and said, No.

"There's going to be an inquest and one of your superiors has already overruled you. That should make it real easy for you.

"Seeing her laying there, my hand resting on her shoulder, I had not planned the next part but it would cap everything nicely—*do what I had to do. I'd do it to her slow and easy.* I leaned over her, looked straight into her eyes and said, where can I find a pair of scissors?

"Her eyes rolled, her head turned slightly. I nudged the silencer into her chin.

"There... in the drawer... the bedside table, she said barely audible.

"I opened the drawer. How handy, I thought.

"While still hovering over her, I said, Now, my dear, just keep your hands by your sides and don't move, not a quiver. You understand? I shoved the barrel into her chin a little harder.

"Yes... Yes, I understand. Her brown eyes were open wide.

"I took the scissors and nudged the gun into her chin a bit harder before cutting the cleavage and two thin straps to lay her bra open.

"Oh God, no no, she whimpered.

"You hush and lay real still, I repeated as I pushed the gun into her chin again."

Karen squirmed in her chair without ever taking her eyes off of him. She remembered the garage, the headlights of the car and the way those men had stripped her as she envisioned what Tina Mathews must have felt.

"I cut through her panties twice and pulled them from under her. I leaned over her face and said, open your mouth, my dear. I poked the remnants deep into her throat. She began to struggle. I slapped her and pushed the gun into her nose. You know I can hurt you bad."

Again Karen fidgeted, listening, hanging on every word.

"I knew that hurting her too much might make her retaliate. The Doc was strong. I'd have to push her just enough.

"I waited and did nothing. When she fidgeted or whimpered I'd push the gun harder into her nose and let her feel the point of the scissors at her neck. The minutes passed, as I sat quietly stroking her thighs—not allowing her to move. The perspiration broke out on her body.

"Her eyes followed as I moved away to pick up my flashlight. You owe me one, Tina. Don't make me come back. I'd really like to do you. I wouldn't call the police either. If you do, I'll know to come back real soon. I turned to leave and then, looking back and focusing the light on her I said, you have a nice dog and then added, you can take the gag out now.

"I walked out of her bedroom and down the stairs. Her pooch lay not far from the front door pressing the ham bone firmly to the floor. My pistol coughed once.

"I heard her scream, Oh No. She raced down the stairs.

"Again, I pointed my flashlight at her as she squatted, hugging her dog, the tail wagging.

"Now you owe me two, Tina. The inquest is just two days away."

Listening—hanging on every word—Karen said, "She disappeared two days after the inquest."

"It was a Friday, just two days after the inquest. About four-thirty, I received a call from Bowers telling me that she was working late and her husband was still in Hutchinson, Kansas. Bowers instructed me to arrest her and bring her to pier 19. He said to use her car, go to her house and pack some clothes and then dispose of everything so they'd never be found.

"I was there, near her car, when she came out of her office. I think she recognized me when I tried to cuff her. She was so terrified I had to shoot her on the spot. I put her body in the trunk and drove to pier 19. I think the Senator and Bowers were disappointed when they learned she was already dead."

"Just like that."

"It wasn't hard. The last time I saw her, Bowers and Donovan were carrying her aboard a runabout."

"A runabout?"

"A cabin cruiser, twenty feet long, I assume they rented it. Donovan had not acquired his yacht yet. Even then they frequently partied together. On that night it was just the two of them."

"You killed her and they dumped her?" Karen said.

"That's the way we did it."

"And the car?"

"There are many places to dispose of stolen cars and I knew all the best ones. After picking up some things at her house I sold it for $100 with instructions to break it down immediately for parts."

"You don't seem to have any reluctance in telling me all this."

"I see you on TV most every day and you seem okay. Donovan's dead and I never liked Bowers. He's a fat wimp. The Senator saved me from the death sentence but I don't owe

Bowers anything. I'd probably like the break of another trial if they try me again."

"Don't you have any remorse?"

"A life is a life, Miss Dyer. When it's over, it's over. The person doesn't know anything then. It's over.

"What if it were your life?"

"When it's over, it's over."

"Did you ever know D. B. Cooper?"

"You just had quite a bout with him."

"He's the one who told me to check with you regarding Tina Mathews."

"All I know is what I've read and hear on the news. Who is he?"

"Nobody knows."

Andrew Phillips smiled. "He's good at what he does. I like him."

~~~~~

Mike was in his office when Karen knocked at the open door and entered. "I'd like to go to Ariel this coming Saturday for the D. B. Cooper celebration. It'll be big this year."

He stood up and circled his desk to greet her. "All the networks will be there. I've been wondering when you'd bring it up. How much staff and equipment do you want to take?"

"None, KOSI will be there with their equipment. Let's make it a holiday, just you and me. We'll rent a car and drive down the west coast after it's over with no itinerary."

"I've got a better idea. There's a ten-day cruise leaving Vancouver, Canada on Sunday going south to Mexico."

"You've been thinking about it too."

"I've been planning on it. The brochures are here on my desk."

"Let's take it both ways, south to Mexico and then back to Vancouver."

# The Celebration

The turnoff to Ariel, Washington was a sharp right that Karen and Mike would never have seen if she hadn't been watching for the small sign with an arrow that read, **ARIEL**. Having just been there a few weeks ago, Karen's recall was fresh. After the sharp right the road made an immediate left sloping downhill paralleling Route 503 for 500 feet. The store sat on the north side of the Lewis River, a tributary feeding into the Columbia River. Built on a steep bank fifty feet above the water, a large sign near the top of a gable spelled out ARIEL STORE, HOME OF D. B. COOPER DAYS in red white and blue block letters. The storefront with the high gable was covered with wood shingles painted blue. An open porch with a tin roof extended two thirds of the way across the front.

With winter just around the corner, the Saturday after Thanksgiving in Washington was cool, the sky gray more often than sunny. On most days there was rain or at best a light mist with the smell of autumn in the air. Today, however, seemed to be magical with the sun at its' zenith illuminating a bright blue sky as if to proclaim announcements with profound wisdom.

Three media vans were on the scene with their dishes in place, looking skyward, collecting and sending material. The KOSI van was just off to the side of the store.

A hand-carved sign to the right of the entrance at eye level was painted blue with red block letters:

ARIEL STORE
"HOME OF D. B. COOPER"

The entry door was red with a glass pane. The doorframe was white.

By the time Karen and Mike arrived, the place was crowded with people elbow to elbow. Karen had chosen to wear a light blue skirt and sandals with a beige blouse and a white kerchief tied around her neck. Mike was casual with a tan shirt and matching slacks.

Inside, D. B. Cooper memorabilia jammed every available place—the walls, the shelves and hanging from the ceiling. Baseball caps, pencils, pictures of what D. B. Cooper may have looked like—all keepsakes for people to buy.

Karen knew Biff Roberts and three other FBI agents would be present, investigating whom D. B. Cooper might be, hoping he couldn't stay away from such an event. The case was far from closed. She wasn't surprised when she saw Chief Oran Biskbey and Sheriff Grant Taylor standing together. Taking Mike by the arm, she said, "Come on, Honey, let's say hello to them." She saw the smile on Oran Biskbey's face as they approached.

"I hoped you'd be here."

"You knew we wouldn't miss this, Oran," Karen said with a hug, remembering to call him by his first name.

"Yes, I guess I did," he said extending his hand to Mike as she turned to Grant Taylor with a hug.

"You think Cooper'll be here?" Karen said.

"I doubt it," Grant said. "You'll meet people here who have claimed for years to know who he is but we haven't been able to build a case on any of them."

"Just like before, he got away and left no trail," Oran said with a grin and looking at Karen with a glint in his eye.

"Excuse me," Grant said. "Somebody just came in that I want to say hello to." He made his way toward the door.

"That's Ted Bolan and his wife, Molly," Oran said. "You may have heard of him."

"No, I haven't," Karen said.

Ted Bolan was wearing a light blue sport shirt open at the neck with a gray jacket and dark blue slacks. Molly had a tan suit with a skirt ending at her knees and a white blouse.

"Most everybody in these parts knows Ted and Molly," Oran said. "He's an ex-CIA agent and he was on the Tacoma city council for eight years. Today he flies around the country in his airplane."

≈≈≈≈≈

Anna Song, an attractive reporter with KATU Channel 2 in Portland was set up and ready to interview Dona Elliott when the word was passed to be quiet and listen. Karen and some other people moved in closer toward the bar to watch. Mike and Oran Biskbey stayed back.

Karen knew of Anna Song even though KATU was not affiliated with CBS. She was an up-and-coming local reporter in Portland. Dona Elliott's name had appeared in the reports that had passed across Karen's desk in the last four weeks. Dona was seated on one of the bar stools. Her son, Jack, stood beside her. A floodlight illuminated the area as the camera focused on Anna. A hush came over the store as the interview began:

"Ladies and gentlemen, we are in the midst of an annual festive occasion commemorating the famous D. B. Cooper. Here to tell us more is the owner of the Ariel Store, Dona Elliott and her son, Jack."

The camera panned away from Anna Song to Dona and Jack. Karen could see the viewfinder on the side of the camera from where she stood.

"How long have you owned the Ariel Store?"

The camera zoomed in on Dona. "Sixteen years."

Karen judged her to be about fifty-five. She had a stocky build. Jack must have been about thirty and just under six feet—blond hair.

"And this is your son?" Anna Song asked gesturing toward Jack.

"Yes, he and I run the store."

"Ms. Elliott, do you believe D. B. Cooper survived in 1971?"

"Yes I do. We hear both stories. A person can make a case to support whatever they choose."

"How could he have disappeared with no trace?"

"He could have come down in the water and been carried to the Columbia River and then washed out to sea."

"I understand they found almost six thousand dollars ten years later," Anna Song said.

"That's the strongest argument for those who believe he didn't make it. He may have been unconscious or drowned in a tributary. They think some of the money floated out of the canvas bag that night. The authorities have never figured out how the money got to the place where the child found it."

"The Child?"

"An eight year old boy named Brian Ingran found it under some rocks."

"But you believe he made it?"

"Oh yes, the authorities didn't know the spot where he jumped for two weeks. He landed, gathered up his chute and walked out."

"But, the money they found, how can you explain that?"

"Nobody knows. He may have landed in the water and some of the money got away. The weakness in the *floating out to sea theory* is that these tributaries have many places where there is quiet water and virtually all of the debris floats to shore rather than going on down stream. It's ten miles to the Columbia River and another seventy miles to the open sea. They would have found something."

"You said they didn't know where he jumped for two weeks. Tell us about that."

Dona Elliott must have told this story hundreds of times in the sixteen years she has owned the store, Karen thought. Her words just rolled out.

"On the flight from Seattle to Reno the airliner performed a slight curtsy right here over Ariel when he jumped."

"I understand that all airliners now have a peep hole in the door to see into the passenger compartment."

"Yes, they were installed after D. B. Cooper jumped."

"So you're convinced that he survived. Do you think the same man stole the money two months ago?"

"No!" Dona Elliott said emphatically. "We know that D. B. Cooper would be in his seventies today. That thief is infringing on the good name of D. B. Cooper."

Turning to Dona's son, Jack, Anna Song asked, "What do you think about this?"

"I agree with Mom. He got away. This Cooper is a fake."

# Karen Knows

When Anna Song finished the interview the noise level increased as people resumed their conversations. That's when Karen noticed Molly Bolan standing a few feet away ordering a drink from the elderly gentleman behind the bar.

"May I have a Pepsi please with lots of ice?" Then, speaking to Karen, "what would you like? I'm buying."

"Thank you. I'd like a Coke," and then added, "with lots of ice." Two men moved away from their bar stools toward the door. "I don't think those men are coming back. Let's take the stools," Karen said.

"It will feel good to sit," Mrs. Bolan said. "I'm Molly Bolan."

"Yes, I know. Grant Taylor pointed you out a while ago. Have you been coming to these celebrations long?"

"We haven't missed many in the last fifteen years since Ted retired," Molly said. "I was raised in this area."

"Then you were here when D. B. Cooper jumped?"

"Just two miles from here."

"Oran Biskbey said your husband was on the Tacoma city council for eight years."

"We still live in Tacoma. Ted was raised there."

"Then he has always lived in Tacoma."

"No, we lived in New York City until Ted retired from the CIA. Ted and I met you once at a Rotary meeting when you were the featured speaker. I almost feel like I know you because we see so much of you on TV."

"How did you and Mr. Bolan meet?"

"Ted has always liked to hunt and fish in this area and I always liked the outdoors. Our paths just happened to cross."

"Sounds like love at first sight."

"My whole life opened up with Ted."

The elderly bartender set a can of Pepsi and a Coke on the bar with two tumblers full of ice. Reaching across, Molly Bolan laid a five-dollar bill on the bar.

"Thank you," Karen said as she poured her Coke over the shimmering ice. "Your husband sounds like a man who has a lot going for him."

Mrs. Bolan smiled. "Yes, too much sometimes. He can't say no to anything."

Karen snickered. "You look like a lady who may have the same attributes."

Molly Bolan poured her drink and took a sip. "Yes, I guess we're both that way."

"When were you married?" Karen asked.

"In January, 1972."

"Oran Biskbey told me you have an airplane."

"Ted was a Navy pilot in World War II."

Karen felt hands at her waist. It was Mike. He had moved in close beside her.

"I'll take a Coors Light," Mike said to the bartender. Then, looking over Karen's shoulder, "Hello Mrs. Bolan."

"Why don't you call me Molly, that's so much nicer?"

"This is Mike and I'm Karen."

"It's nice to meet you, Molly," Mike said, moving in beside Karen. "I was just talking with your husband." Then, speaking to Karen, "they have an airplane, honey. He flew B24 Liberators as a Navy pilot in World War II."

"I know, Molly told me."

"He's a ventriloquist and does a lot of impersonations," Mike added. "Grant told me he makes his own dummies and speaks frequently in support of the Bolan Foundation."

"The Bolan Foundation?" Karen said.

"The VFW created it in Ted's name," Molly said.

"He might make an interesting guest for you," Mike said.

"Yes, I think so."

"Karen, I could write a book about the things my husband does."

~~~~~

For the next hour Karen circulated among the guests. As Dona had said, many of the old-timers claimed to know who D. B. Cooper is and, in some cases, even pointed to a person.

Mike was in the general store area. Karen was standing at the bulletin board. Articles describing D. B. Cooper's escapades written and published over many years were tacked or stapled haphazardly. Many clips were placed on top of one another three and four deep.

A section of the board had lots of snapshots taken from previous years. She spotted a picture of Ted Bolan, Molly and Dona standing in front of the bar. Karen pulled it off the board for a closer look. They were standing and it was a good picture of Ted Bolan. She thought of the night of the shooting, she didn't know why. She replaced the picture on the board.

Karen saw Ted Bolan moving out through the entrance. It was the first time she had seen him alone since she and Mike had arrived three hours ago. She followed him out of the store onto the drive. The late afternoon sun peeked through the tall pines.

"It has been a fun day," Karen said as she approached him. "Lots of interesting people."

"Yes it has," he said, turning to face her.

"I'm Karen Dyer," she said extending her hand.

"I know who you are. You have been a favorite with Molly and me for many years. You haven't been doing any interviews."

"No, Mike and I decided that this was going to be a day to watch and meet the people."

"Everybody knows who you are."

"Ha, speak for yourself, Romeo."

He laughed. "Molly and I have been coming to these celebrations for years. She was raised here."

"Yes, she told me."

"She's the best thing that ever happened to me."

Karen knew the voice. His posture, the picture she had just seen on the bulletin board. D. B. Cooper jumped in November 1971 and they were married in 1972. He had been a Navy pilot. Dummies—the old woman in the car. Ted Bolan is a master of disguise—a man of many voices—the way he interrogated Lewiski. The CIA, that's how he knew about Andrew Phillips and the leads that involved Steve Bowers and Roger Stark. Both of them will be indicted for murder. She was sure of that.

Karen knew the whole story now—everything. Molly had been part of the conspiracy in 1971 when she met the man. It was all so simple. They returned to New York City and he resumed his career as a CIA agent. He said he met me at a Rotary meeting in New York City. Molly had just confirmed this. *Ted Bolan is D. B. Cooper.*

Looking straight at him, she said, "I'll take that Barbi Doll anytime you call."

"We do have a common bond, don't we?"

They both smiled. She couldn't resist giving him a hug with both arms and whispering, "I'll never tell, not even, Mike."

"Nor will I tell Molly."

≈≈≈≈≈

The ship wasn't large, only 484 passengers. The brilliance of the morning sun created beams of light into their stateroom. Mike and Karen had just shared their first night on board. They were lying close with her head nestled on his shoulder.

"You know," Mike said, "there is only one thing we have learned for sure about D. B. Cooper."

"And, what is that?"

"We know there are two D. B. Coopers."

"Honey, the only thing we know is what he wanted us to know."

Lightning Source UK Ltd.
Milton Keynes UK
05 November 2010

162448UK00001B/49/P